W9-BVA-622

THE GIRL THAT VANISHED

A.J. RIVERS

PROLOGUE

ONE WEEK AGO

Her phone never rang after ten. The world might still be churning outside, but in the little white house at the end of a winding brick path, everything stopped as soon as the clock ticked past nine. So, when her phone started ringing at almost midnight, it took Sandra a few seconds to process the sound. It seemed to ring from a far distance, somewhere she wouldn't be able to find it. But as the fog of sleep dissipated, it sounded stronger and louder, finally leading her to snatch it from the bedside table where she left it when she toppled into the sheets hours before.

"Yes?" she muttered, rubbing away the sting in her eyes with her fingertips.

"Mrs. Brooks?" a voice asked.

"It's Ms."

The correction was a reflex. Four years after her bitter divorce, Sandra still felt like she was fighting to reclaim herself. People always assumed she was still attached to him. The 'r' was implied, a given to most people who spoke to her. It was just a letter. Just one tiny letter.

But it made so much of an impact. Even in her almost-sleep, she snapped back against it even before she could fully process the voice speaking to her. It sounded familiar in that distant kind of way that she knew she'd heard it before, but no face formed in her thoughts.

"Yes?" she repeated.

"This is Troy Macmillan, from Twin Rivers Camp."

The mention of the summer camp she sent her daughter to just three days before snapped her awake. Sitting up against the headboard, Sandra turned on the lamp beside her and squinted at the sharp pain the bright light cut through her eyes.

"What's wrong? Is Alice homesick? Let me speak to her," she said.

It was the first time she let her daughter go away from home for more than a few hours. At ten years old, she hadn't even had a sleepover with a friend from school. She preferred to be at home, to lose herself in her world of books and dolls, her pets and her mother. This summer was meant to be different. Sandra saw glimpses of change in her daughter, hints that she was right on the brink of breaking out of her shell. Securing her a spot at the idyllic summer camp for the first two weeks of summer break was meant to give her a nudge. Sandra envisioned her daughter coming home at the end of the two weeks brimming with confidence and stories and wanting to fill her schedule with new friends and activities.

But now it seemed that after just three days, Alice wasn't coping. Sandra had prepared for this. She wasn't going to force her daughter out into a world she wasn't ready for and possibly end up making her retract even more. She told her to give it a couple of nights, and if she wasn't having fun to call her. Sandra was readying herself to give Alice an encouraging talk when the camp director finally responded.

"No. Alice is missing."

Sandra didn't know how she got to the camp. She was just suddenly there, dressed and with her thick hair pulled back in a clip that pressed painfully into the back of her skull. The yellow glow from the windows of the administration building was jarring against the velvet brushstrokes of the darkened landscape. It was still hours from sunrise, but she wasn't going to wait for it to get to the man who said those words to her. She didn't remember putting on her clothes, sweeping back her unbrushed hair, or driving the thirty minutes outside the town limits. But she would always remember the ominous light of the building.

The door opened before she got to the top step, and some of the light spilled out onto the porch. A dark-haired man wearing yesterday's clothes and tomorrow's fear stood in the doorway waiting for her. He stretched his hand out to her, but Sandra didn't take it.

"Where is my daughter?" she demanded. "What happened to her?"

"Please, come inside," Macmillan said, backing into the building.

She followed but didn't take the seat he offered.

"How could my daughter be missing?"

"She was accounted for at dinner, and then went to the evening activity at the recreation center. We had a campfire tonight, and her cabinmates say she was there and then went back with them for bed. She was in her bunk at lights out, but when one of the other girls woke up to use the restroom, she noticed Alice wasn't in her bunk," Macmillan explained.

"How long ago was that?" Sandra asked.

"About an hour before I called you."

Heat burned across her cheeks and down the back of her neck as spots danced in front of her eyes.

"An hour before you called me? My daughter has been missing for almost two hours? Where are the police?"

"Sometimes girls leave their cabins for dares, or because they want the excitement of breaking the rules. It's happened many times before, and we find them wandering the woods or trying to meet up with boys at the boathouse."

"She is ten years old," Sandra said through gritted teeth.

"We looked for her throughout the camp, and when we couldn't find her, we called you. We wanted to make sure you knew what was happening before we moved forward. Just in case there is a history of her running away or sneaking out."

Her hands could have snapped his desk in half. She took a step toward him and leaned so he could see the bloodshot lines in her eyes. She wanted him to hear her words. To know what she meant by them.

"You lost my child. Get the fucking police here now."

CHAPTER ONE

NOW

"I know it isn't real. But for the first few moments, it feels like it is."

"Every time?"

My lungs depress as my breath slides out of them.

"Yes."

"What does that feel like?"

I try not to resent the question. She's doing her job. I'm the one closing off to it.

"Horrific," I tell her. "I thought in dreams you weren't supposed to be able to experience your senses. That's what separates the perception of a dream from reality."

"That's a common belief, but the more we look into how the brain functions during sleep and what dreams really are, the more we're learning that the brain is capable of some extraordinary things. Many people can't feel any sensation during dreams, but for some, the intensity of experience in a dream is no different from being awake. Some even report the sensations are more intense, including physical pain."

"So, that whole 'somebody pinch me' thing is just a bunch of bullshit," I mutter.

The therapist looks like she wants to laugh, but it would be unprofessional. Instead, she adjusts her glasses up her thin nose and nods.

"That's a good way of putting it. Especially in situations that are dramatic or impactful, your brain can relive every aspect of it in dream form. This seems especially true for nightmares."

I nod.

"I can tell you that's true. Even when I've realized I'm dreaming, everything is clear. I can feel the cold on my skin. I've never felt cold like that. Which doesn't make sense because I know I've been in colder places. I've *lived* in colder places. But that night was cold like every cell of my body was turning to ice. And the smell."

My eyes close as I try not to let it take over me right now. "The house smells like decay and dust and death. I can taste it. I don't want to breathe because it gets on my tongue and makes me gag. I don't want to go into the basement. Every time I have the dream, in those few minutes before it sinks in that it's not real, something still tells me to stay away from the basement."

"But you still go. Even when you realize you're having a nightmare and what's waiting for you down there, you still go. Why?" she asks.

"Because I have to. That's the only way I can explain it. I have to go. I'm walking through that house, and I know exactly where I am. Even more than I did when I was actually there. He told me so much when we were up in that bedroom, and it all comes back. I can see him growing up there. I can see what his parents put him through. I don't know if that makes me want to go further because I understand the progression, or because I want to get away from all the images. Either way, I just have to keep going."

"So, you blame others for what happened?" she asks.

The question takes me aback, and I blink at her a few times. I'm not lying down on a couch the way I thought I would be when Creagan told me I had to go see the therapist. Not that the concept of talking to a counselor is totally foreign to me. You don't see the things I've seen in the field without having your mind combed through a few times. But before now, my experiences have been visits in my office or group talks with other members of the team. This is the first time I've been involved in structured therapy just for me, and I went into it with the Hollywood vision. I saw myself stretched out on a couch staring at the ceiling while the therapist sat with a pad and paper behind my head. I'd stare up at the ceiling and contemplate inkblots while I let my brain catch back up to reality.

It isn't that way. The office is brightly lit and devoid of any heavy wood and dark leather. The couch where I sit is dusty pink with navy throw pillows that I sometimes hold in my lap just because they're there. Maybe that's why she put them there. Not really to add any visual appeal, but as a clandestine hugging mechanism. I'm clutching one hard now as I wrap my head around what she just asked.

"What?" I ask. "Why would you say that? Who would I blame?"

"You said you understand."

"What?"

"You said you understand," she repeats.

"I understand the process. I understand what brought him to where he got. That doesn't mean I understand what he did or let him off the hook for it. He is to blame. But he's not the only one."

"Who?"

My head cocks to the side as I search her eyes, trying to get on the same page as her. I feel like I'm missing something.

"What?" I ask again.

"Who do you blame?"

I narrow my eyes at her. I feel like she's playing games with me, and I don't like it.

"I just said, I blame him. His parents and his siblings contributed to the mindset that brought him to that point, but he is to blame for what he did. Especially the first murders," I tell her.

"Do you realize you haven't said his name at all? This is our sixth session, and you've avoided saying his name every single time."

"His name is Jake," I say slowly.

The name tastes bitter coming out of my mouth. I remember all the other times it tumbled across my tongue and the feelings it once stirred. Everything stings more when I say it.

"And when you walk through Jake's house and go down into the basement, what do you find?" she asks.

"My mother."

"Alright."

She says it in that elongated, leading way that tells me she wants all the details, even the ones I don't want to share. That's why I'm here, though. So she can crack me open and strain what's inside.

"She's with the other bodies. The sub-basement looks just like it did when I was really there. All the bodies are in their positions, arranged into the different scenes. Christmas, a board game, dinner. It's all just like it was when I found it. But when I get closer, I realize there's an extra scene, and my mother's body is in it."

"What's she doing?"

"Reading. She's stretched out on a chaise lounge, reading a book. Her feet are bare, and I'm worried they're cold. I want to cover them up for her. But I get closer and see the skin is discolored. When I look at her face, her eye sockets are empty. I didn't notice the eyes of any of the bodies when I was there. I guess I should have."

"Why?"

"I always notice eyes. It's just something about people I always look at. You can tell a lot about a person and what they're thinking just by looking into their eyes."

"You certainly can," she nods. I immediately wonder what she sees in mine. "In the dream, how do you feel when you see your mother?"

"Horrified. Is there any other way I should feel? She's been dead for so many years. She always wanted to be cremated, so the last time I saw her was in an urn. Then I'm standing there looking at her corpse, and all I can think about is what was done to her to get her there. She didn't just die. That would have been horrible enough. But she was murdered, just like the rest of the people in that room. She was ripped away from me, taken by someone who had no right to do it. Only it's different. For all those other people, their justice is coming. We know who killed them and he's going to answer for it. My mother doesn't have that. And we don't have it for her," I say.

"Does it bother you that she was cremated?"

"That she was cremated?" I ask.

"Some people have a hard time with the decision of a loved one that wants to be cremated. They don't like the thought of the physical body being destroyed and the loss of the opportunity to see it after death. Is that something you've struggled with since the death of your mother?"

She's walking alongside me into my dream now, standing beside me as I look at my mother. But she doesn't see her the way I do. She's not looking at her. She's deconstructing that I see her, dismantling the nightmare that haunts me like seeing the structure will take away the power. The magic trick isn't magic when you know the magician's secrets.

It won't work that way. She could pick apart every image and compartmentalize the seconds, giving each one a neat explanation, and it wouldn't matter. I don't care why I see her. Only that I do. Only that I always will.

"She always wanted to be cremated. It wasn't a surprise. Her parents were cremated when they died, and she brought their ashes to the U.S. when she left Russia. Their urns were always on the mantle or a table in the living room. She always used to say they never got the chance to get to America when they were alive, so she wanted them to be able to watch her live their dream. It's not like I was shocked when that's what she put down in her final wishes," I shrug.

"Your mother recorded her final wishes? She was very young to do something like that, wasn't she?" she asks.

It's a stark reminder of how distant this woman is from me. She was given only the most basic of briefings when Creagan funneled me into her office and everything else she's having to construct from what I give her. I'm building the mountains she wants me to climb over.

"With my father's line of work and our lifestyle when I was younger, it didn't seem that strange. They both made out living wills the same day they got their marriage license."

"About your father... do you ever see him in your dream?" she asks.

9

I shake my head. "Never."

"And Greg?"

"No. They are both missing. Not dead."

She nods and looks down at the tablet in her lap. The stylus poised between her fingers takes the place of the pen I envisioned her holding. She occasionally sweeps it across the screen when I say something she finds is notable.

"You told me before your father wasn't around much when you were younger," she leads.

"No, I told you he frequently had to leave home for work. It wasn't uncommon for him to be gone for a few days or weeks, sometimes even a couple of months at a time. I never knew where he went or why. He needed to go, so I accepted it."

"Is that what you thought was happening when he disappeared nine years ago?"

"Ten," I correct her. "It will be ten in a few days. And, yes. That's what I thought was happening. I thought it wouldn't be more than a few days. A week at the most. Then I realized it was something much more. I haven't heard from him since."

"How about Greg? Did he go away like that, too?" she asks.

"No. He was the most dependable, predictable person I ever knew. He never left without telling me exactly where he was going and how long he would be gone. That was never more than two days. When he disappeared, there was no warning and no explanation."

"You mentioned the two of you ended your relationship shortly before he disappeared. If the two of you were no longer dating, why would you expect an explanation for why he was leaving?" she asks.

There's an accusatory note in her voice, faint behind the words and hidden more by her not lifting her eyes to look at me when she asks the question. It doesn't affect me. It's not like this is the first time I've had someone ask that, either in words or in the way they looked at me. I know why they ask it, but I don't care.

"I didn't expect an explanation. Him disappearing is even stranger *because* he broke up with me. It's like he knew it was going to happen and didn't want me involved. That's why I'm still looking for him."

"That's why you went to Maine recently," she says.

"Yes. There was a tip that suggested he might be there, so I went to follow up on it."

"But you're not actually involved in the investigation."

"No. As a matter of fact, I've been specifically told not to interfere. Which is why I went for the weekend on my own dime."

"And did you find anything?"

I let out a breath.

"No. The tip didn't pan out, and I don't have anything else to go on right now."

I'm relieved when the virtual assistant positioned on the corner of her desk tells the therapist our time is up. She calls out to it to tell the alarm to stop as she stands and extends her hand to me in our customary end-of-session handshake.

"I'll expect you the same time next week?" she asks.

"No. I'll need to reschedule our next session. I'll be out of town for several days next week."

"Oh?"

She wants me to give her more of an explanation, but I'm not going to. I sling my bag over my shoulder and give her a small smile.

"I'll talk to the receptionist and figure out the best day."

I leave the office, tell the receptionist to email me with a rescheduled appointment, and walk out of the building into the bright June sun.

CHAPTER TWO

THEN

If she closed her eyes and concentrated enough, she could almost smell the hints of her birthday cake still lingering in the air. They were the same vanilla-laced, chocolate-studded notes that clung to her father the last time she breathed him in. She always had two birthday cakes. For as long as she could remember, she would have one to celebrate with whatever friends or family she might have nearby when her birthday came along, and another just to share with her father. The first was doled out in neat slices and careful portions. The second eaten with fingertips and mouthfuls, wayward forks chiseling away whenever one of them passed by the counter. They set it between them on the couch while they watched movies and justified it for breakfast.

He smelled like the last chunk of cake he stuffed under the edge of his coffee cup as he balanced it on a chipped bread and butter plate. Her mother always wanted him to throw that plate away. She was embarrassed by the chip and thought it made them look bad that it stayed nestled among the rest of the dishes in the cabinet. Sometimes she snatched it up from the sink and dropped it into the trash can. He would wash it carefully and tuck it back in place, telling her it was still good, it shouldn't be wasted. It became a joke between them, a playful thread of consistency they carried through no matter where they ended up. Many things got left behind in the times they had to run, but never that plate. It weathered every shift, move, and sudden change.

They kept it then because it made them feel closer. She kept it now because it was her turn.

She watched him carry that plate into his tiny office two days after her birthday, right before leaving for one of her summer classes. She found it there the next day. She got home late the night before and hadn't seen him all morning, so she went in to check. She stood in her father's office, breathing in the lingering energy of her party, staring at the plate and the crumbs of cake. The mug and the cold coffee. She wrapped her arms around herself and searched for the warmth of the sugar-nuanced hug he gave her before she left.

He had left already. Something caught his attention and lured him away. He was expected somewhere, needed by someone. She knew he would be back. She had seen this before.

She let the plate sit there for another three days before cleaning it up.

She didn't start worrying for another three days.

That's when the envelopes came. Sitting among the rest of the mail like an innocuous circular or 'to our friend at this address', they seemed like nothing. They were anything but.

She recognized the handwriting packed tightly on the front of each one. It was the faceless lawyer her parents always worked with. She'd never met him but heard his name and saw his handwriting. This time it formed her name. Sitting on the couch, the remnants of her birthday cake wrapped tightly in foil and tucked in the freezer; she opened the envelopes. One by one, the structure of her father's life slipped out onto the table.

The deed to the house signed over to her.

An acknowledgement of her car loan paid off in full.

Notices of credit cards and other accounts closed.

Receipts from large pre-payments made to the utility companies to cover many months of service.

Gift cards to several stores in the area to cover groceries, clothes, gas, and other necessities.

Notices of her college tuition paid in full for the next three years.

His marriage license.

Her mother's death certificate.

Papers for a bank account holding a considerable amount of money, enough that it seemed her parents saved from before she was born to squirrel it away.

There was nothing to explain any of it. No letter, no note. No contact information for someone to tell her what was happening or help her when she might need it. Just the pieces of a life that now seemed like it didn't even exist. She sat and stared at the papers until the sun was gone and shadows made the house feel cold even with the summer heat outside. When she finally looked away, everything seemed different. The house, a place she had started to think of as home after her father actually bought it, unlike all the other ones they ever lived in, didn't look the same. It didn't feel the same. But it was hers.

It was hers, and it never felt more foreign.

Barely a week beyond her eighteenth birthday, she was alone. The house her father bought so she could stay home while she went to college belonged to her. Her car was paid off. Her tuition covered. A bank account brimmed with more money than she imagined having until well into adulthood. Her life was set up for her, but she was at the edge of facing it by herself.

That's when she knew he was gone. It would be a while still before she fully accepted it as her reality enough to say it to other people. But that was the moment she would look back on as when everything in her life changed. It would go on. Life always went on. It had to. But in so many ways, it stopped then.

Part of her was still eighteen years old, waiting for her father to come home and finish her birthday cake.

CHAPTER THREE

NOW

"How did your session go? Did she find all the gears that need polishing up in that brain of yours?"

I shoot a glare at Eric as he laughs and pushes away from the porch column so he can follow me down the steps of the therapist's office.

"You are so supportive," I roll my eyes at him.

"You know I'm just kidding. I think it's great you agreed to see the doc after everything you went through the last few months."

"'Agreed' is probably a bit of an overstatement," I tell him, settling my sunglasses into place and sweeping my blond hair up and off the back of my neck.

I've only been outside twelve seconds, and the steamy heat of a Virginia summer is slicking sweat across my skin.

"Alright. I think that it's great Creagan forced you to see the doc after everything you went through the last few months. Is that more accurate?" he asks.

"Closer."

"It's good for you, Em. I know you don't like talking about things, but sometimes you have to let people help you."

"I know. Which is why I'm still going. I just wish she would stay focused."

"What do you mean?"

We walk down the sidewalk toward the parking deck. The therapist's office is close enough to the main office complex where we work that I didn't bother to drive. Scheduling my appointments for right after work means I can just walk over and then walk back to my car. It makes wedging the meetings into my calendar seem like less of an intrusion.

"Creagan sent me there because of what happened in Feathered Nest. He thinks I need help getting through that experience and the trial," I explain.

"Which you do. Anyone would," Eric nods.

"Then why does she keep trying to wander off into talking about my parents? Or Greg? I mentioned them the first appointment with her because I was trying to explain what was going on leading up to me going undercover, but she keeps going back to them."

"I guess she thinks they have more of an impact than you do."

"But that's the problem. I can't even connect the dots. There are these big glaring holes even I don't know how to fill. So how is she possibly supposed to pick them apart and analyze it?" I ask.

"I don't know," he admits. "Just, Emma…" he pauses, and I turn to look at him. "Please try."

"What do you mean?" I frown, starting to walk again.

"You know what I mean. You've gone through more in the first almost twenty-eight years of your life than most people do in their entire life, and you let it get to you. You weren't yourself when you got banished to desk duty, and I don't think you were fully back when you went to Feathered Nest. You were in a bad place, and it seriously affected you. Some of the things you did and decisions you made…"

"I know, Eric," I interrupt, pushing the button for the parking deck elevator. "I've had a few months to think about it."

"And you're going to have to keep thinking about it. Until the trial is over…"

"Even when it is over, I'm going to keep thinking about it," I reply. "It's never going to go away."

"No, it's not. Which is why you need to work through it. Don't push against her. It could have ended much worse for you there, and I don't ever want to feel that fear about you again."

The elevator opens, and I let out a long breath before stepping out.

"I'll try harder," I promise.

"Good."

We walk across the mostly deserted floor toward my car, where I parked it in the same place I do every morning. I surreptitiously peek under it as I walk around behind it and glance through the back window. It's a habit I picked up in college and have found myself drifting back to since getting home. Eric doesn't mention it, but I see his eyes follow the path of mine like he wants to confirm my car's safety for himself.

"What are you doing here, anyway?" I ask.

I open the back door and toss my bag onto the seat.

"Can't your best friend wait encouragingly for you to make sure your therapy session went well without you being suspicious about it?" he shrugs.

I narrow my eyes at him across the roof of the car.

"No," I tell him.

He gives a dramatic sigh, his shoulders sagging.

"I've been sent to collect you and bring you..."

"No surprise parties," I say, opening my door.

"Bellamy has been planning..."

"No. Surprise. Parties," I repeat, getting into the car.

Eric quickly opens the passenger door, knowing full well I am not above driving off with him still standing there.

"Emma, your birthday is tomorrow."

"As I've been reminded by various restaurant email newsletters I don't remember signing up for and my eye doctor who sends the same birthday card-slash-appointment reminder with a big owl every single year," I tell him. "I'm not surprised by it and don't need to be surprised by a party, either."

He reaches over and latches onto the steering wheel before I can start driving away.

"I know better than anyone else you don't like to celebrate your birthday. That's fine most years. Not this one. Bellamy and I came far too close to losing you earlier this year, and we both think the fact that we didn't is worth celebrating. So, with every ounce of patience and love I have in me, I'm telling you you're going to stop arguing, drive to my place, put on the outfit Bellamy picked out for you, and then go to your house for the party she snuck in to throw for you."

"Well, that was forceful," I mutter.

"You didn't leave me much of a choice."

I roll my lips in to stop myself from laughing.

"Wait. Did you say she snuck into my house?" I ask.

"Yes. Moving right along."

He gestures through the windshield like he's directing me to leave the parking deck.

"How did she expect you to convince me to change my clothes without you giving away the surprise?" I ask.

"I don't think she thought that far ahead," he offers.

"Where is your car?"

"She did think far enough to bring me to work this morning."

I pull out of the parking spot, and Eric reaches forward to turn on the radio. One of the lessons from my father I've carried with me since he taught me to drive was not to have the radio on in the car. As he put it, getting too wrapped up in the chorus of one song could end in being wrapped up around a tree. Not exactly the image I like having on my mind when on the road. Eric, however, is one of those people who seems to think the radio is in the car because it's a critical component of an internal combustion engine. He always has to have something playing if he's in the car, even if he's not driving. This time he compromises by settling on the news rather than music. It picks up at the beginning of a report.

"Three days after the mysterious disappearance of 10-year-old Alice Brooks, police are no closer to finding the fifth grader from Sherwood," the reporter says.

"Sherwood," Eric repeats. "Isn't that the town you grew up in?"

I nod. "As close to it as I got."

"*Brooks disappeared during her first week at the Twin Rivers Summer Camp,*" the report continues. "*Fellow campers say she attended all the evening activities as planned and was in her assigned cabin when they all went to bed. At some point within the next hour to two hours, Brooks either left or was taken from the cabin. A cabin mate discovered her absence and brought it to the attention of counselors. Camp director Troy Macmillan is cooperating fully with police and provided full access to the camp, facilities, and surrounding areas for investigation. Sandra Brooks, the child's mother, has been working actively with the investigation. If you have any information, please contact local law enforcement.*"

A chill runs down my spine, but I force it away.

"I hope they find her," Eric says.

"I'm sure they will," I tell him. "That summer camp has been there for generations. The last time I was in Sherwood, there were people I knew whose grandparents went there. There were a few times when kids would go missing because they wandered off into the woods on some dare or just got turned around. It's easy to do. They always wound up wandering their way back into camp, or the search parties found them."

"Sounds like the counselors need to do a better job of keeping their eye on the campers," Eric says.

"So, is this one of Bellamy's famous themed parties? I just want to know what I'm getting myself into," I say, trying to push the conversation past the disturbing news report.

I let what I told Eric carry away the heavy thoughts. It was true. I didn't have long blocks of uninterrupted years in Sherwood the way other people do in their hometowns, but it's the nearest thing to an anchored, firm home I ever had. Even Florida doesn't have the same type of attachment. I loved my time in Florida and still dream of the shade of palm trees and the sting of concrete on my feet even though I've been away for so long. But being there always felt like a visit. Sometimes extended to many months, but still a visit. I haven't been in Sherwood in many years, but I know what it feels like there. I carry memories of there that feel like mine. It's the difference between a postcard and a diary.

Among those memories are tense summer days when TVs and radios churned out reports, much like the one we just heard. A child at the summer camp is missing. They're doing everything they can to find them. They were upsetting reports to hear, but they always resolved themselves. We never left Sherwood with a child not safely with their family.

It's going to be the same this time. They'll find the little girl, or she'll manage to find her way back to the trail that heads into the camp. A news story will run celebrating her safe return and giving a stern warning for children to follow rules and not get themselves into dangerous situations. Parents will hug their children a little tighter, and some may hesitate on sending them to camp for the next summer. Soon, it will all be back to normal.

CHAPTER FOUR

I planned my trip specifically around the goal of not being in town for my birthday and getting to glide by without it being acknowledged. I should have known the effort was going to be wasted. If Bellamy had any say, she would make it a law for people to not only acknowledge their birthdays but to celebrate them with appropriate enthusiasm. That alone makes me want to hide from my best friends every year as the days leading up to my birthday dwindle. I would just as soon let the day pass like any other. Not since my eighteenth birthday have I had any interest in celebrating.

But it turns out I shouldn't have been so resistant to the idea of Bellamy throwing me a surprise party. She kept the merriment subdued and the bursts of confetti and glitter to a minimum. Though several people from work were there for the initial shouting of *'surprise!'*, they didn't stay for long. For most of the evening, it was just Bellamy, Eric, and me. The three of us sat on the couch and ate from the massive spread of party food she set out while watching movies. Like everything was normal. Like my ex-boyfriend didn't break up with me and disappear. Like my parents weren't gone. Like I never went undercover in Feathered Nest.

I use a black permanent marker to write the year on an aluminum-wrapped wedge of cake. It joins the others in my freezer. It used to be I would stumble on one of the slices while digging through the food in the freezer and tuck it back into the corner. Now there is little room for anything else in half the small freezer.

The house is quiet now that Bellamy and Eric have left. He sat in her passenger seat, both staring straight ahead like they're convincing themselves the space between them hasn't gotten smaller, that the months haven't chipped away at the strain that has always existed between them. In the quiet, my mind goes back to the session with the therapist and how she trod on ground I fiercely protected.

Creagan sent me to counseling to help me through what I experienced a few months ago. I didn't expect her to ask about my mother, to question her cremation like it meant something more. It felt like she discovered a hidden place in my thoughts and pried it open, revealing what I hid from everyone, even from myself. I hate that my mother was cremated. I hate that the last time I saw her was beneath a sheet on a stretcher. She was the most beautiful woman in the world. I just wanted to touch her face one more time.

Heading back into the living room, I drop down onto the couch. The second everyone left, I was in pajamas with my mascara scrubbed off. Now all I want to do is stretch out on the couch and wait for sleep. It's been harder to find it recently. Days go by where I'm only able to snatch a few disconnected hours over the course of the entire night. Some nights, those hours dilute down to bare minutes, and I wander into work the next morning feeling like I'm walking through Jell-O.

Sometimes I know that type of night is coming. Somehow, I can feel it, like the potential for sleep is disappearing from my mind and muscles even before I've gotten near my bed. On those nights, I've found taking up residence on the couch rather than the bed can make a difference. As if I can trick my brain into thinking I'm not going to sleep when I sit down in the living room and can sneak up on it.

The cream-colored chenille blanket draped over the back of the couch and a pillow subtly tucked into the space beneath one end table come out just as my eyelids start to droop. There's not much room to stretch out the long frame gifted to me by my mother on the couch. I usually greet the morning with more than a few creaks, pops, and groans as I try to release tight muscles. But I'll trade an hour of full range of motion for enough sleep to function any day.

Nestling into my favorite corner of the couch, I feel something prod me in the back. I reach into the crack between the cushions and the side of the couch and pull out a small white box. I don't recognize it, and the plain sides give me no hint as to what it might be or why it's in my couch. Prying off the top, I find a folded notecard.

"Happy Birthday," I read.

There's no signature or indication of who it's from. Under the card is a bundle of purple tissue paper tied with a narrow lavender satin ribbon. I untie the delicate bow and unfold the paper. Nestled in the paper is a necklace. A round silver pendant swirling with translucent colors dangles from a thin chain. With a puzzled frown, I reach for my phone and call Bellamy.

"Hmmm?" she answers, through the sleep that obviously doesn't elude her.

"Did you sneak a birthday present into my couch?" I ask.

"Did I what?" she asks.

"A birthday present. Did you sneak one down into the cushions of my couch?"

"No. I gave you the picture frame because I got too busy organizing the party and forgot to get anything else."

It also came with a handwritten IOU for a more thought-out gift in the future. Bellamy is not known for being smooth when it comes to covering up her mistakes.

"And Eric gave me the antique lapel pin from Florida." I think back to the handful of other guests and the gifts they gave me. "Who could this be from?"

"What is it?" she asks.

I describe the necklace. "It's definitely intended as a gift. The note says happy birthday. But the box wasn't wrapped, and there's no name on it or anything."

"And it was on your couch?"

"Not even on it. In it. Like stuffed down beside the cushion. We've been sitting here all night and didn't notice it. I only found it because I went to lie down."

"Well, it must be from someone who couldn't make it but sent a gift with someone else. I'm sure they'll mention it at work," she offers.

"Alright. Let me know if you hear anything. Good night."

She mumbles something, already partway back to sleep, and I set my phone back on the table. A few seconds later, it rings again. Assuming she suddenly remembered who left the gift, I answer it and hold it to my ear without looking at the screen.

"Who was it?" I ask.

But only silence comes through the phone. "Bellamy?" Still no response. "Did you roll over on your phone?"

A slight crackling noise precedes what sounds like a soft breath. It's not the disturbing deep breathing everyone has seen in a thousand movies and thinks actually happens all the time. It's light and almost trembling, like the person on the other end is trying to either pretend they aren't there or are trying to work themselves up to saying something.

"Hello?" I say.

The line clicks. I look down at the screen in confusion. I don't recognize the number, and there's no name attached to it. I pull up the search engine and type in the number. The results make my hands feel cold, and my lungs constrict. It's from Feathered Nest.

My fingers twitch, wanting to call the number back. I hesitate. The person on the other end of the line called but didn't say anything. It's possible it was a mistake. A strange and cruelly coincidental mistake, but a mistake that shouldn't necessitate an awkward exchange with me calling back. But it could also be something more. Just because they didn't say anything doesn't mean there weren't words there waiting to be said. It was just too difficult to get them out.

After barely ten seconds of internal debate, I give in to my curiosity and dial the number back. It rings several times before going to a generic voicemail inbox. I call again to the same effect. My third call goes directly to voicemail as if whoever it is has turned off their phone to avoid having to look at my number pursuing them. I leave a message and slip the phone back onto the table in front of me with a heavy sigh.

Pulling the blanket down off the back of the couch, I curl up beneath it and try to focus on the familiar old movie on the TV. I've seen this one so many times the lines go through my mind without me even having to try to remember. It's comforting in its predictability and the way it floats past without my thoughts having to give any effort to keeping up.

But tonight I can't let myself drift away in it. My mind keeps wandering back to the phone call. My eyes wander to the jewelry box on the table and the edge of the note sticking up out of it. I pick it up again and look at the words on it. *Happy Birthday.* That's it. Nothing else. I let my gaze trace the curves of the letters and break them down into individual lines. I take in their slope and spacing, trying to identify them. They look almost familiar. I try to dig through my memories to come up with why I know them. It must be someone from the office who I've worked with enough to have read their notes, but not enough to instantly recognize their handwriting.

That doesn't really narrow it down a ton.

When the end credits roll by with my eyes still open, I give up my attempt to go to sleep and head into my bedroom. I'm not leaving for another two days, but I yank out my suitcase anyway and start packing. It's something to fill the time, and when sleep finally does catch up with me, I won't have to worry about snatching an empty bag off the carousel after I climb off the plane.

Traveling is far from an unusual concept for me, which means I have a full stock of toiletries ready to toss into my carry-on. I add them in along with the change of clothes, pajamas, gum, and snacks that always populate my bag after an incident with lost luggage a few years ago. Opening the zipper on the inside of the bag, I tuck in a small bag and promptly close the pouch. With nothing else to do to prepare for the trip, I go back to the couch and finally fall asleep.

CHAPTER FIVE

I should have taken a shower before getting on the plane from Des Moines. Usually, that's the last thing I do before checking out of a hotel and heading home. This time I decided to shave that out of my schedule in favor of hiding under the comforter and trying to maintain my grasp on sleep that, just as I predicted, finally caught up to me.

Staying asleep meant I didn't have to think about the disappointing few days I spent in Iowa. But it also means I feel grimy, stuffed in the window seat of the economy airline gliding toward the ground. Planes already tend to leave me feeling a little germ-coated. It's an inevitability when traveling in such a close space with a couple hundred other people.

Hours in a plane leave me feeling uncomfortable on a good day. Without a shower, I just feel sticky.

The bounce of the wheels on the tarmac is a relief, and I pry my hand away from the armrest. I'm not a fan of landings. The plane glides toward the gate, and I reach for my bag where I shoved it beneath the seat in front of me. As soon as the plane stops, the other passengers stream out of their seats and into the narrow aisle. There's always something fascinating about watching people try to hurry out of a plane. It never works. No matter how forcefully they wedge themselves into the rush squeezing out of the single door, their feet will likely hit airport carpet at the exact same moment they would have if they had just waited for the chaos to end and walked out calmly.

And yet, I do it too.

Bumped back and forth by the people in front and behind me, I perform the plane shuffle out through the accordion tube and finally make it into the terminal. Now to get my suitcase and get home. I'm halfway down the steps when I notice my name scrawled on a white sign held up in front of a man's face. It might have startled me if I didn't know the rest of the body attached to that unseen face. It's Eric. He's my official ride to the airport whenever I travel, and if he has the chance when I get back, he picks me up.

This is at least the tenth time I've seen a variation of that sign. I'm sure people think there's some sort of hilarious or touching story connected to why he always holds up my name when I deplane and come down the stairs toward him, but there's not. He did it the first time he picked me up, and it just never changed.

I adore this man.

"That's me," I tell him like I always do.

He drops the sign and grins at me.

"Your suitcase is looking for you," he says. "I'll bring you to it."

"Thanks. It is so impatient."

He slings an arm around me as we start toward the baggage claim.

"So, that's not the face of someone who made life-changing discoveries during her visit to Iowa," he observes.

I let out a sigh and shake my head.

"No, it is not."

"Need a drink?" he asks.

"I need my couch. But I won't turn down the drink in conjunction with that."

"Let's go have a beautiful luggage reunion, and then we'll see what we can do," he says.

I'm a little more thankful for Eric every time I leave the airport without having to join the throng of people gathered around the rental car counter, going to battle over the taxis, or playing ride-share roulette. I get to stroll past them and slip into a familiar, comfortable car driven by someone I actually know. It's one of life's little luxuries I never lose sight of, no matter how many times it happens.

The drive back to my house takes just over an hour, and he refrains from asking me any more questions about my trip. Instead, he plugs in his phone and plays a stream of his eclectically mixed music. When we get to my house, I head directly for the shower.

Eric is waiting in the living room with a bottle of rum and two glasses. He knows this isn't a dignified bottle of wine situation. This is a soak me like a fruit cake conversation. Not that I've reached a point where I need to drink myself into oblivion. Just one where I'd like to dull a few of my sharp thoughts and make some questions forget about themselves.

He offers up a glistening glass to me as I settle into the corner of the couch and lean back against the arm to look at him. We touch the rims of our glasses together and take simultaneous sips.

"Alright," he starts, setting his glass on the table. "What happened? Give me the full Iowa rundown."

I take a second sip, steeling myself for the distinctly not thrilling story I have to tell him.

"It's very quiet. And there's a lot of corn," I tell him.

"The scene-setting is inspiring. What about the field?"

"The Field of Dreams?" I ask. "As in, the movie filming site, the dead man who was apparently good friends with my parents wrote down as his address at the hotel he checked-in to, the day he died on my front porch?"

"Well, you got bitter really fast," he says. "I thought the rum would mellow you out."

"I'm sorry. It was just so frustrating." I reach over and set my glass on the table next to the necklace box. "I went there hoping... I don't even know what I was hoping. Was it completely ridiculous for me to go there?"

"No. He knew your parents. It might have been a long time ago,

31

but he knew them. That means he might have known something about who killed your mother or where your father is. It's not ridiculous to chase after anything you might be able to find. It's been a long time. If there's any chance of you finding out something about either one of them, you should go after it. No matter where that is," he tells me.

I stare at him, one of the two best friends who have seen me through everything. Eric knows me better than anyone, in some ways even better than Bellamy, and he's never judged me. That's a lie. He judges me constantly. But in the ways that I need to be judged. He's there to tell me when I've gone off the rails or am making a bad decision. He's there to tell me when I need to take a step back from something and look at it a different way. But he's always there for me. Whether I listen to him or not, he's there.

When I give him the chance to be. I haven't this time. Not completely. He knows the man showed up dead on the front porch of the cabin the Bureau rented for me in Feathered Nest on the first night I was there for my undercover assignment. He did the research when I questioned the name the man wrote on the registration card at the hotel. Ron Murdock. It wasn't his name, though I haven't found one yet to replace it when I think of him. I told him about the hotel and the strange fake address he gave, about the surveillance camera footage of him checking in. Eric found me the picture of the man with my parents.

But I've been hiding something from him. The first piece of the puzzle that told me this was more than just the accident the police wanted me to believe it was. I kept it to myself. From the moment I found it, I didn't show it to anyone else or tell anyone it existed. I should have. It was compulsive and arrogant to keep it tucked away, but it was what I thought was right at the moment. Now I have to share it.

"I'll be right back," I tell him.

"Emma?" Eric calls after me. "Are you okay?"

"Just give me a second."

I go into my bedroom and open the drawer in my nightstand.

The book tucked there is the same one I've had there since I was young. It was my mother's favorite, and after she died, I found it in the spot where she last read it. Since then, I've read through it at least once a year and kept it beside my bed. Now it has another purpose.

Gently opening the book, I take out the piece of paper tucked in the spine. I do my best to smooth it out, but it still shows the wrinkles and lines from being clutched so tightly. A single drop of blood darkens one corner of the paper. I stare down at my name for a few seconds before putting the book away and bringing it into the living room. Eric has gotten through his first glass of rum and is refilling it when I sit back down on the couch. He looks at me strangely.

"What's that?" he asks.

"You need to let me get the whole story out before you react," I warn him.

"It's always good when you say that."

"Just... let me talk." I wait until he nods in agreement before I continue talking. "The first night I got to Feathered Nest, someone knocked on the door to the cabin, and I thought it was the guy who owned it coming to check on me."

"I know. Then you opened the door, and the dead guy was on your porch."

"I thought you agreed not to talk," I deadpan to him.

"Go ahead."

"I leaned down to check his pulse and noticed something in his hand. It was this." I hold up the paper. Eric takes the note from my hand and glances down at it. He looks like he's going to burst, so I jump in before he has a chance. "I didn't show the police because I was undercover. This has my real name on it, and they'd realize I wasn't who I said I was. It would have completely compromised the entire assignment. Then I decided not to tell anyone because, like you said, I've been doing this for a long time. I've been trying to understand my mother's murder and my father's disappearance for so many years. I didn't want anyone to try to stop me or get in my way when this could be the thing I've been waiting for. This man could be the link I've

33

tried to find that might actually tell me what happened. I couldn't risk someone, anyone, deciding to butt into it."

"Do I get to talk now?" he asks.

"Yes."

"What in the hell were you thinking? You were undercover. No one was supposed to know you were there except the Bureau. Then a man shows up dead on your porch with your name written on a piece of paper in his hand, and you keep that to yourself? Look, Emma, I understand how much it means to you to find out what happened to your mother and to find your father. And Greg."

"This has nothing to do with Greg," I snap with more intensity than I intend. "This isn't about him. I want to know what happened to him, of course. I want to know where he is and that he's safe. But that's completely separate from my parents."

"Alright. It's not about Greg. But it is about someone who shouldn't have known where you were at all showing up dead in front of you when you had barely even gotten there. Did it never sink in what that could have meant? Or how much danger you were putting yourself in? How much danger you were already in?"

"I understand, Eric."

"Do you? Emma, you have made some seriously questionable choices in your career…"

"Eric, I know. I didn't show you this to give you a reason to lecture me. This was not a great choice; I get that. But this had nothing to do with the case I was on there, and it would have gotten in the way. That man, whoever he is, was there for me. Not because I was in Feathered Nest and not because I was investigating the disappearances. He was after me, and I didn't want either one of those issues to muddle the other. Can you honestly tell me if I had handed the note over to Chief LaRoche when I first found it, he would have done anything? That it would have made any difference at all?"

"It might not have. But it's been months."

"And the investigation into his death is closed."

"With his death deemed an accident, which you know damn well it wasn't. They don't even know his real name," Eric points out.

"So, we're on level grounds there," I tell him.

"He might have a family. People who would want to know he's gone."

"Eric, if he has a family, they already know. Just like every time my father walked out of the house, there was a part of me that thought he might not come back. If he hadn't, I would have known."

Eric looks at me, his eyes a mixture of softness and anger.

"Listen to what you're saying, Emma."

I realize it without him having to point it out to me. My father did walk out of the house and not come back. And I haven't just accepted him being gone. I've fought for years, never stopping my search for him. But I can't bring myself to think of this man, the one who I can only call Ron Murdock because I haven't found anything else to give me another name, has anyone wondering the same thing about him.

"He had no identification, no legitimate address, no luggage. They didn't even find a car that could have been his. If he does have a family out there and they are wondering where he is, I'm sorry. I feel horrible for them because I know what they're going through. But I'm not going to regret holding this back. This piece of paper proves there's more. I'm not just searching for ghosts."

CHAPTER SIX

"This is why you had me research him. You knew I was going to find something that had to do with your parents."

His voice sounds almost accusatory, and I know there's a part of him that feels betrayed. I should have included him in this from the beginning. But I couldn't. Eric does things by the book. Like all of us, he has occasionally drifted off the path of the straight and narrow when the situation warranted it. There are always extenuating circumstances and situations that don't fit into the mold. But this wouldn't have been one of them. Concealing evidence was something he never would have gone along with. He would have made sure it got into the hands of investigators, and now I can already tell he feels like everything has gone off track. It might not have been the safest choice or the most ethical choice, but it was what I had to do.

"I didn't know that for sure. How could I? All I knew was this man had my name on a piece of paper, and nobody knew who he was. But now I know he did have something to do with my parents. Not that that did me a lot of good chasing him to Iowa."

"What did you do while you were there?"

"I went to the address he put on the registration card. It really was the Field of Dreams. I looked around there for a while, but there wasn't anything. I showed his picture around to everyone that I found. People who were there, people in all the hotels and restaurants and gas stations within a fifty-mile radius. Nobody recognized him. Of course, I was showing them a picture of him from twenty years ago, but they didn't even seem like they thought they might recognize him. I did as much research as I could. I looked through town records, but they were only available for the last few years. The rest are kept in archives, and I had to request access to them. I won't know if there's anything to find out until I can go through them, but if I don't even know the man's name, I'm not going to know if I found out anything."

Eric holds up the note.

"Why are you showing me this now? I know you're saying you had some sort of fit of conscience and wanted to come clean, but come on, Emma. I know you. You're not just going to have a confessional moment because it makes you feel better. You've hung onto this and not said anything about it for months. There's a reason you decided now was the time for you to take it out and show me. What is it?" he asks.

I let out a sigh. I adore this man and kind of hate him sometimes, too. But he's brilliant and extremely good at his job, so I'll put up with the rest for now.

"It doesn't make sense," I admit.

"What do you mean?" he asks.

"The note," I explain, taking it from him and looking down at it. "The picture you sent me had this man looking very friendly with my parents. They looked like they were friends for years and knew each other extremely well. Why would someone who knew me as a child need to have my name written on a piece of paper when he came to find me?"

"He didn't necessarily know you," Eric says.

"I was eight years old when that picture was taken," I point out.

"Right. But just because he knew your parents doesn't mean he knew you. There are probably a lot of people who think they knew your father, and many of them would have different stories about who he is and what they know about him. He was always protective of you. You've always told me that. It wasn't lost on him how dangerous his life was. He was a smart man, Emma. He knew who he was and what he was doing. He wouldn't want to put you at risk. It's possible this man knew your parents but didn't meet you," Eric offers.

"Okay. So, if he didn't know me, why come after me? How did he know who I was? And where I was undercover?" I ask.

"There's something else we haven't considered. He might have known you, even if you didn't know him. We are working under the assumption that he wrote your name on that piece of paper. Think about it. It's just your name. Nothing else. Not where you are staying, a description of you, your phone number. Nothing but your name. He might not have written it. He might have taken it from someone else."

"I can't believe I never thought of that," I tell him. I open my computer and pull up a folder of archived pictures. From it, I select the image of the registration card the man filled out at the hotel. Enlarging the picture, I hold the note up beside it and compare the handwriting.

"They aren't the same. The note doesn't look like just natural handwriting. It's almost like someone who's used to writing in cursive forced themselves to write in print. The registration card is in print, too, but it's more relaxed. The same person could have written both of them. He could have consciously tried to make his writing different, but I don't know what the point of that would be."

Eric shakes his head in agreement. "I don't know. But it's something to keep in mind."

"I still don't understand the address. There are plenty of other cards that didn't have the address filled out," I say. "And even if he didn't realize that and was going to put down a fake address, which I can get, why wouldn't he just make something up? Why choose the Field of Dreams?"

Eric shrugs. "If you build it, they will come."

I look at him. "What?"

"If you build it, they will come," he repeats. "The movie?"

I shake my head. "I never saw it."

"You never saw *Field of Dreams*?" he asks.

39

"Baseball wasn't exactly one of my passions growing up. The only reason I knew that's what the address was is because it popped up in the results." Eric looks even more confused, and I search his face. "What?"

"It just makes the whole situation make even less sense," he explains. "If the movie meant something to you or to your parents, or if your father loved baseball, or... anything, it would make sense."

"Why would that make sense? Why would he think I'd ever find the address?"

"What do you mean?"

"I found the address because I looked at his registration card. He had no reason to think I was going to do that. Why would I? He was coming after me, not the other way around. Why would he think I would end up looking at his address?" I ask.

"Unless he knew he was going to die."

E ric's words are still sitting heavily in my heart when the combination of the rum and many long, hard days at work starts pulling on his eyelids, and I tip him over to lay his head on the pillow and stretch across the couch. It's not late enough for sleep to even be on the horizon yet for me, so I decide to unpack while he rests. I head into the bedroom and pick my suitcase up from the floor. Turning to my bed, I notice something I didn't before. A small stack of mail is sitting on the blanket, close to the pillows. Creeping back into the living room, I grab my phone and call Bellamy.

"You home?" she asks.

"Yep. Got here a while ago, but I've been talking to Eric. Thanks for bringing in my mail. I appreciate it," I say.

"I didn't bring in your mail. Oh, no. Was I supposed to?" she asks. "Was that sarcasm?"

"No," I say, reaching over to touch the stack of mail. "That wasn't sarcasm. You didn't bring in my mail?"

"No."

"I'll call you back," I say.

The line clicks before she says anything, and I let the phone drop to the top of the bed. My hand shakes just slightly as I pick up the envelopes and folded circulars. Bellamy is the only person who has an extra key to my house. No neighbors. No strategically placed lawn ornaments. Eric doesn't even have one. Only Bellamy. But someone else got in.

I slowly flip through the mail. Bills. A birthday card from Creagan. Junk mail. But in the middle of the stack, I stop. The plain white envelope has no address, no stamp, nothing but my name. The handwriting looks instantly familiar. I bring the envelope with me back into the living room and snatch up the necklace box, taking the note out of it and letting go of the rest. It falls to the table and skitters across the surface to tumble over the edge onto the floor. The sound jostles Eric, and he opens his eyes. He didn't sleep for long, but it was enough to take the edge off his tiredness, and he pulls himself up to sitting.

"What's wrong?" he mutters through a groan and rubs his eyes.

"Look at this," I say, holding the envelope and the note out to him.

"Where did this note come from?" he asks.

I explain finding the jewelry box in the couch cushions.

"I thought it was probably just someone at work, and I didn't recognize the handwriting right off. But look. It's the same as the envelope. Bellamy says she didn't bring my mail in, but it was sitting there on my bed, and this was in it."

"Did you open it?" Eric asks.

I shake my head. "Not yet."

Sliding my finger under the sealed flap, I open the envelope and take out the thick folded piece of paper inside. It's only folded in half, and I lift the top. The words inside, in the same handwriting as the note from the necklace box, make my blood run cold.

Where is he?

CHAPTER SEVEN

Eric's eyes burn into me. I can feel him staring at me before I even turn to look at him, and I know what he's thinking.

"Emma…" he starts.

I nod, stopping him.

"I know. Go ahead."

He picks up his phone and calls the police. I can hear the dispatcher's voice through the line and his responding, but don't register the words. My world has shrunken down, focused in, so there's a tunnel around the paper in my hand. I set the birthday note and the new letter down on the table and use my fingertips to draw the paper with my name on it over beside them. Lined up for comparison, I look at them together and then individually. I isolate the letters, my mind pulling them up from the paper, and transposing them onto the other pieces of paper so I can see if they fit.

They aren't the same.

"Officers are coming," Eric says when he gets off the phone.

He looks down at the papers I'm comparing.

"The handwriting doesn't match," I sigh. "Obviously, it would take an expert doing a more in-depth evaluation, but…"

Eric puts his hand on my back to quiet me. I'm spiraling, burying myself in the technicalities of the case, and the cold, stark procedures of work rather than letting myself experience what's actually happening. It's happened before. Everything built up inside me as I pushed it down, shoved it away where no one would see it, until it cracked and spilled out, threatening lives and cases.

I can't let that happen again.

"I don't think you need to show them the note with your name on it. I don't think it has anything to do with this, and it would just confuse things more," he says.

"Are you suggesting I withhold evidence?" I ask, grateful for the brief moment of levity.

"I'm counting myself lucky you agreed to get the police involved in this at all. I'm not going to rock the boat. But I still think, at another time, you need to show that to somebody. It could mean more than you think it does."

I nod but don't directly agree. I know how Eric feels about transparency and doing things the right way. It's why I didn't give him all the information when I asked him to look up the dead man in the first place. It's not that I wanted to lie to him or deceive him in any way. But he just doesn't understand. It's not his fault. It's not that he doesn't want to see this from my perspective, but he can't. He'll never be able to fully grasp what this is like for me and what it means. His childhood was easy and predictable. When he's told me about it, he says that like it's a bad thing. He doesn't see the comparison. He doesn't know that I peer into the looking glass of his eyes and see predictability with wonder. Possibly even envy.

Eric never questioned anything about his family or his place in the world. He never had to run in the middle of the night or wake up not recognizing the ceiling over his bed or the blanket pulled over him. He doesn't have a list of stories chronicled in his mind, contradicting each other as they offered a series of explanations to death and disappearance. He can trace his life. There are no gaps in his mind where he doesn't remember where he was or what he was doing. His parents appear in all his memories. He went to school in the same places and graduated with the same people rather than jumping from schools to tutors and graduating alone over a computer screen.

He's never going to understand. But he doesn't have to.

The police arrive with the exact attitude I expect from them. They smirk at the notes, nod condescendingly at the explanation. It's nothing to them. Another overzealous person who has watched too many crime shows and has injected themselves into a storyline. They don't realize they're playing right into it. The questions come right out of a script.

"Are you sure your door was locked?"

"Did you post your travel plans on social media?"

"How many neighbors have extra keys?"

"Do you keep a key under the doormat?"

"Were any of your windows open when you left?"

"Could you have forgotten bringing in the mail yourself?"

"Who is the 'he' the note is talking about?"

That one grates at me. The others were annoying, even offensive, but understandable. The last one creates instant, irrational anger in me.

"If I knew that, you wouldn't be standing in my house right now," I tell them through gritted teeth.

One looks at me, and I'm reminded of the slimy look in the eyes of Nicolas, the young officer I butted heads with in Feathered Nest earlier this year. It carries the same dismissal, the same arrogance. He sees a woman who can't manage her own problems and probably got herself into them in the first place. He wants me to sit down and let them handle it without question.

Eric's hands on my shoulders don't calm me.

"You'll have to excuse her. She's been through a lot recently," he says.

I shrug away from him and take a step closer to the officers.

"No. I don't need them to excuse me. I do need them to understand they are here for one reason and one reason only, and that is to make sure they're aware of what's happening now, so when I find out who's playing this sick little game, they aren't surprised by the consequences."

"She's... the federal agent who took down Jake Logan," Eric says with a sigh, finishing the thought he started. I pull out my badge and offer it as proof.

The name registers with the officers, and they stand down. Their posture changes as they evaluate me in a completely different light. My face has stayed out of the media. I haven't done any interviews, and the Bureau has shielded my identity to protect me and preserve the integrity of any future undercover work. But it's customary for those types of safeguards to be let down when interacting with law enforcement. Considering the chain of custody has likely put Jake in their paths at some point during this phase of his trial, clueing them in will give them a bit more insight into my state of mind. And possibly the gravity of these notes.

"Jake Logan?" one asks. "The..."

His eyes flicker to me, and I nod.

"Serial killer. They haven't given him any sort of fancy moniker yet. Thank god."

"Do you think this could have anything to do with him?" the other officer asks.

"Considering he's been in custody since that night, I highly doubt it was actually him. But as you can imagine, it puts me a bit more on edge. Serial killer fetishes are very real, and the people who fall for these guys are intense. If there's a leak somewhere and someone figured out who I am, it could get twisted pretty fast. I called you to establish a record. If anything else happens, there will already be a history, and it will be easier to respond. With things like this, the individual incidents might not seem serious or even like they're related at all, but if you have an established pattern, they stand out."

"We'll process the house and set up some surveillance," the first officer offers.

"Thanks. I'll be in town for a few more days, but then I'm taking a vacation. Part of it I plan on spending here, but I'll also be traveling," I tell him.

"We'll make sure someone is keeping an eye on the house when you aren't here. In the meantime, you might want to consider relocating to somewhere else until you leave for your trip. Just to get you out of the environment."

I shake my head adamantly. "No. I appreciate the concern, but I'm not going to let a couple of notes chase me out of my home. If anything else happens, we'll consider the option, but for now, I'm staying here. Like I said, I just wanted to establish the record."

The officers walk out of the house to make calls and start processing the scene. I know that means roaming around the house inside and out, looking for vulnerabilities and entrance points, looking for anomalies. They'll try to pinpoint how the person got in and if anything else was left or changed. I can only imagine how my neighbors are reacting to all this. Despite the years living here, I haven't gotten close with any of them. It's easier not to. The idea of taking a jaunt across the lawn to get a cup of sugar and gossip over coffee is quaint, but it's too close. I don't want to share my past with more people, and it's exhausting veiling it. The cordial smile and wave when we pass by each other are enough.

"Maybe you should come stay with me," Eric says. "Just for a couple of days."

"No, Eric."

"Then stay with Bellamy," he suggests.

"No. You heard what I said. I didn't call in the cavalry to rescue me, and I'm not going to run away and hide until someone catches the Boogey Man for me. This could be nothing."

"And it could be something very serious."

"It could. And if it is, I'll handle it. For now, I've let the police in on it. They know what's happened so far and are going to keep an eye on the house," I tell him. "I have a lot to think about right now with the hearing tomorrow and whatever turn the case is going to take. And after that, I'm really looking forward to some time off."

"Just promise me if anything else happens, anything at all, you will let me know. You won't try to take this on by yourself," he pleads.

"I promise."

CHAPTER EIGHT

"Tell me again how you met the defendant."

Alvin Roderick, a lawyer I've watched stroll through more than enough courtrooms in my life, walks past me and gestures at the defendant table like he's asking me to bid on a prize on *Price is Right*. I don't want my eyes to follow his hand, but they do anyway.

The man sitting at the stand is a stranger. Somewhere in the deepest recesses of me, I know it's Jake. But it's not. Laughing crystal blue eyes have faded to gray. Long hair I once longed to run my fingers through cut short. His hands folded together on the table remind me of when they held mine. They felt safe and protective then.

Now I know what those hands are capable of.

"I met him when I went on an undercover assignment," I say. "He owned a bar in the town where I was investigating."

Roderick nods and continues to pace. It's a tactic of his. It's supposed to put the person on the stand on edge, but it just annoys me.

"And what were the details of that undercover assignment?" he asks.

"To investigate a string of disappearances and murders that occurred there over the last two years."

"And was your investigation successful?"

"If you want to put it that way, yes. I found the person responsible for the crimes," I answer.

"In fact, that's the reason we're here, isn't it? Because you believe the defendant, Mr. Logan, is the one responsible. Isn't that right?" Roderick asks.

"Yes."

"And how would you describe your relationship with Mr. Logan? Friendly?"

"Yes. Until it wasn't."

"How about romantic?" Roderick leads.

"Yes," I admit.

There's no reason to try to hide or put a spin on it. This is just the beginning. More hearings, meetings, and testimonies will follow. Everything is going to come out. What little hasn't already. Pretending it wasn't exactly what it was won't do any good. But I'm under no delusion it won't be used against me. The attorney wouldn't ask about it if it wasn't.

"Yes," he repeats, nodding toward the jury with a secretive smile like they're sharing something. "As a matter of fact, the truth is you and Mr. Logan became very close almost immediately upon meeting and were engaged in a personal relationship for the entire time you were in Feathered Nest."

"We became friends, and that evolved into a more romantic relationship," I confirm.

"Miss Griffin, how long have you been with the FBI?"

"Almost six years," I say.

"And you are how old?" he asks.

"Twenty-nine."

"Which means you entered the Bureau at twenty-three. That's the minimum age for an agent, isn't it?"

I don't bother to withhold my sigh of frustration. We're not getting anywhere, and I'm sure his twirling questioning will just get worse.

"It is," I confirm.

"You must be a very worthy candidate."

"I worked extremely hard in school and excelled in training."

"So, what you're saying is someone with your heightened awareness and polished skills of intuition had no hesitation entering into a romantic relationship with Mr. Logan," Roderick says.

"Intuition isn't a skill," I point out.

"Fair enough. But you are trained to evaluate people, to scrutinize them and recognize certain characteristics in them," he says.

"Yes."

"And you didn't recognize anything in Mr. Logan that gave you pause? Nothing that made you suspicious? Even someone with your tremendous instincts considered him completely normal?"

"The word 'normal' is extremely weighted. I think there is such a thing as average and fitting with expectation. But I hesitate to describe anyone as normal."

"Very well, Miss Griffin. We won't use the word normal. Is it fair to say you didn't have reservations about him? That you, in fact, trusted him?"

"Yes."

He tosses another look at the jury, this one pretending to be so puzzled he just can't understand what I'm saying to him.

"You met many people in Feathered Nest. Did you form such close connections to any of them?"

"No."

"Did you trust any of them?"

"No."

"So, not only did you not have reservations about Mr. Logan, you actually set him apart from everyone else you met in the town and identified him as someone you could trust and rely on. Is that right?" Roderick asks.

"Mr. Logan is very good at pretending to be the person he wants to be," I tell him.

"A rabbit isn't afraid of a wolf because that wolf isn't pretending not to be mean, Miss Griffin. It instinctually knows to be afraid."

"Are you suggesting every woman should instinctively be afraid of every man, Mr. Roderick?" I ask.

His expression shifts. He wasn't expecting that type of response.

"Of course, that's not what I'm suggesting. But the severity and truly grotesque nature of the crimes does suggest a person of a certain character."

"Let me tell you, Mr. Roderick. Rabbits aren't afraid of wolves because they show their teeth. They aren't afraid of them because they don't like the way they look. They're afraid because it is born into them. Genetic memory tells them the wolf is a threat. Not because there is something inherently flawed or unperceptive about the rabbit. But because that is what nature created. The instinct to fear exists in the animal kingdom because one animal's survival relies on the death of another. The hunt is about staying alive. What separates humans from the animals is necessity. Humans don't have a food chain within ourselves. There is no need to kill to live. There is only the thrill."

I glare directly into Roderick's eyes.

"Man's greatest enemy is man, make no mistake. It's the compulsion to kill without need that makes a human truly terrifying. We may be able to recognize danger in certain individuals, but we cannot have an instinct to fear all who are dangerous because there's no way to know. We are trained to befriend the enemy. To eat with them, rely on them, lie down beside them. There is no division between the enemy and the friend. As soon as a wolf begins to gather the rabbits to protect them as they pass through the pack, you can talk about instinct. Until then, you can only say I am a human being who spent several weeks falling under the spell of a man who convinced everyone around him, he was the last person they should fear. This isn't about believing someone's lies because I have a hard time even saying he was lying. A lie is about deception. He was telling me, and everyone else, what he has taught himself is true."

Roderick has positioned himself, so looking at him means looking at the defendant's table. Jake stares back at me, and the emotion in his eyes makes the center of my chest ache, and my stomach feel like it's going to tear in two. I want to hate him. I want more than I could ever

THE GIRL THAT VANISHED

describe to feel nothing for him, but the hatred and disgust his actions deserve.

But I can't. So much of me does feel those things. But there's another part of me that doesn't just remember the words he said, but the way he said them. I can still see the look in his eyes and the pain in the way he touched the faces of corpses his mind turned into people he loved. That's the part of me that can't hate him. I hate what he did and what he put me through. I hate the chaos he caused and the effects of it that will go on into the future. But I feel pain for him.

Two hours later, I walk out of the courthouse and feel like breath enters my lungs for the first time today. Eric had to leave the hearing for another work assignment, and Bellamy wasn't involved, so I'm alone as I step into a pool of sunlight and lean back to tilt my face up toward the sky. The heat feels good on my skin after the chill of the air conditioner inside. It seeps through my eyelids, creating an orange glow.

"Emma?"

The voice brings some of the tension back to my muscles. I stand up, the bones of my spine stacking back up, so I stand straight and turn toward the man. Chief LaRoche has his hands in his pockets and stares at me through dark-tinted sunglasses. I knew he was here. He was in the courtroom during the hearing but didn't get called up to speak. He will. The time will come for him to talk about his part in all that happened. The months haven't done much to soften my distaste of the man. He isn't who I thought he was, but he's still arrogant, misogynistic, and rude.

"Chief," I nod in greeting.

He takes the few steps up closer to me and pauses like he expects me to say something. Finally, he relents to the reality that he approached me and not the other way around.

"It's been a while," he says.

"It has," I confirm, even though it really hasn't. This is the third time we've been in the same room together since I left Feathered Nest.

"How have you been?"

There's an awkwardness to the question. Like he really wants to say something else.

"Better."

"Good to hear," he says. "You didn't have to spend too long in the hospital, did you?" he asks.

"No. A few days," I shrug. "But there was a lot of healing to do after that."

"I'm sorry I didn't get a chance to get up there to visit you," he says.

"You had done enough."

Despite how I feel about LaRoche, I can't forget it was his team who were there to rescue me after my confrontation with Jake.

"Can I ask you something, Emma?" he asks, and I nod. "Did you really think it was me?"

"Yes," I tell him without hesitation. "There was evidence and compelling circumstances. And, regardless of the little existential fit Roderick had in there, I immediately had a feeling about you. Something that didn't sit right with me. To your credit, Jake had a major hand in that. He did a good job twisting things and pointing them right at you."

"And your bad feeling?" he asks.

"I think we can both agree it wasn't completely unfounded," I say.

His eyebrows knit tighter together.

"I didn't kill anybody."

"But you did have affairs, break women's hearts, and lie about it. You manipulated their trust and used your position as chief of police for your own ends. You hid your connection to Cristela Jordan even after she died when it could have meant something."

"What could it have meant?" he asks defensively. "I had nothing to do with what Jake did to Cristela. It destroyed me when she died. Can't you imagine how hard that was for me? I had to investigate her death. I had to go to those train tracks and look at her body. I had to see what he did to her. And no one knew what we had, so I couldn't show any emotion. I couldn't grieve for her."

"That isn't anyone's fault but yours. You are the one who kept the entire relationship quiet. But that's not what matters. What matters is you didn't say anything. When she went missing and then showed up by those tracks, you didn't say anything about being with her the last night anyone saw her. You didn't tell anyone you knew Jake drove her back and forth."

"Are you saying I somehow should have known he was behind it? I should have just guessed that since he drove her and knew we were together, obviously he was the one who cut her up and sent her running for that train track? You were sleeping with the guy, and you didn't know."

"I wasn't sleeping with him," I say. "But if I was dating someone secretly and they ended up dead, I'd want to make sure the person I last saw them with didn't have anything to do with it."

"I guess it all ended up alright in the end," he mutters.

Except for Cristela and all the people who died after her, I want to say, but I hold it back. Arguing with the chief isn't going to do any good. It won't change what happened or bring back any of the lives that were lost. All we can do now is be satisfied Jake was caught, and his lawyer isn't going to be able to talk his way out of it.

"How is Cole?" I ask.

LaRoche nods. "He's getting there. This was all a lot for him. He's just trying to figure it out. I don't think he knows how he's supposed to feel about it."

"I can't imagine he'll ever really know how he's supposed to feel about it," I say.

"Finding out Jake is his son hit him hard."

"I think in a way he always knew. Or at least suspected it. That had to be why Jake was treated so badly by his family. I find it hard to believe the man he thought was his father wouldn't have confronted Cole about it."

"It would explain a lot of things I heard from my father about those two," he says.

"Can I ask you a question now?"

"Go ahead."

"How could no one know? Feathered Nest is so small. How could no one know where Jake lived or that Wendy was his grandmother?" I ask.

"I told you once, Emma. People keep to themselves. They don't pry into people's lives. Everyone knew John Logan and the way he could be. People tended to steer clear of him. His father was even worse than him, and Jake seemed to be keeping things together."

"So, no one ever thought to check," I say. "They just let him get beaten down until there was nothing left but the dreams that helped him survive."

LaRoche doesn't say anything in response. I give a slight nod. "Have a good day, Chief."

I turn to walk away.

"Emma."

I turn back around and lift my eyebrows at him. He stares at me for another few seconds. "You did well. I wouldn't have had the balls to go into that place alone."

"Thank you."

CHAPTER NINE

HIM

It had been a long time since he was that close to her. It was different from walking through her space or being near enough to where she had been to feel her in the air, to smell her. Then he could sense her. He could feel her distant presence. He could even use images he'd stolen from pictures and etched into his mind as a way to carry them as his own to imagine her there with him.

But now he could see her. She was so close. No more than a dozen yards away. Close enough to see the darker streaks in her blond hair and the glint of a bracelet around her wrist.

Emma. He wanted to say it, to call it out, and see if she responded. But he held it back. Not yet. Not now. As much as he wanted to see how she would react when she saw him, he knew this wasn't the time. His chance would come. Soon he would have his moment, but he had to be patient. If he acted too fast, it could ruin everything. But he'd been waiting so long. So many years.

Questions hung around him. He'd get the answers soon.

For now, he had to settle for hiding behind sunglasses and the edge of a statue that shaded him just enough to conceal his face. Even if she looked his way, he could dip back behind the stone before she got a good enough look at his face to recognize him.

He waited for her outside for hours. He found out the next time she would be there and positioned himself outside that morning, not wanting to risk missing her. The glimpse he got of her as she arrived and hurried up the steps into the building wasn't enough. He settled against the statue to wait. The sun sparkled on the mica and stung on his skin, but he waited. She was worth the sweat gliding down the back of his neck. Worth the heat searing his forearms and burning the tips of his ears. He passed the day on bottled water and picking the grains of coarse salt from a soft pretzel.

He liked unraveling the pretzel, seeing how many of the twists and curves he could separate from each other without it cracking.

The evening crept across the sky and brought relief from the sunlight. He would have stayed even without it. She was worth it. Now he was getting his reward. Emma. She was right there. So close.

Even if he hadn't seen her walk into the building that morning and saw the royal blue suit she was wearing, and even if he couldn't see her face when she walked out, he would know her. She wasn't happy to be talking to the man outside the courthouse. She let him step closer to her and carried on a conversation, but he knew by the way she held herself, she didn't want to be interacting with him. She wasn't afraid or on edge. Just disconnected. She held herself just like her mother had.

Her body was stronger and more athletic than her mother's, but still had the graceful, delicate lines gifted to her by the Russian ballerina's lineage. She was skilled at controlling her face and giving nothing away with her eyes. She could convince anyone of anything she wanted them to believe. But the way she carried her shoulders and the slope of her hip told everything.

He could go rescue her, go take her away from the man in the uniform. But she wasn't ready for that. He didn't know what she would do if she saw him. If he was to just walk up to them and tell the man in the uniform, the police chief, to leave her alone. What reaction could he even expect? There were still too many questions left unanswered for him to know what the moment after she first saw him would bring. Then the next moment. And the next. Still an unknown.

They were just too far away for him to be able to hear what they were saying. He was tracing their facial expressions and watching the way she held her body with each thing she said to him. It didn't look like he was propositioning her or trying to force his attentions on her. And it didn't seem like she was rejecting him or adamantly trying to push him away. But there was a definite intensity in the way they looked at each other and delivered the unheard words. It didn't take a tremendous amount of imagination to come up with an idea about what they were discussing. He knew Emma didn't leave her assignment in his town with a free head and levity in her heart.

She walked away after a final exchange, and he watched the police chief watching her. When she was too far away for him to call out to her without catching the attention of everyone else around, the chief turned and headed back inside the building.

He waited. She was going to the office. It was still early in the day, and she would try to get in as much work as she could before leaving for the vacation she had been lusting after since the day she walked out of the hospital. He was already ready for that. He wouldn't follow her immediately. There was more he needed to do first. But she wouldn't get too far away from him. He knew where to find her.

It had been so long. Everything he wanted had always been just beyond his grasp. Finally, it was getting closer. Soon he would have everything the years had denied him. And Emma. She wouldn't have to be afraid or unsure anymore. She wouldn't have to keep chasing shadows and reaching into nothingness. All the questions she'd been carrying with her for so long would finally be answered.

CHAPTER TEN

My carry-on bag is still mostly packed from my trip to Iowa. I knew I'd be leaving on vacation soon, so there was no point in unpacking things I wasn't going to use in the interim, just to put them all back in. I find the few things I need to add, including the small bag I put in the zippered compartment and put them in the bag, then turn to finish my suitcase. The house is too quiet, so I have the TV on in the background. I'm not really paying attention to what's on, and I don't register any of the sounds coming from it until I hear a word I didn't want to hear on the news again.

"Sherwood."

I hurry into the living room and snatch up the remote. The news is on, and I rewind to watch the report from the beginning. The woman giving the report looks drawn and solemn, not the expression of someone who is going to announce the joyful return of a missing child to her family.

"At the top of the hour, we return to a story we've been watching develop in Sherwood. Police there say there is still no sign of Alice Brooks, the ten-year-old girl who disappeared from summer camp late last month. Despite exhaustive searches of the camp property and her home, teams have found nothing to suggest what might have happened to her or where she might be now. This is particularly upsetting in light of the disappearance of another child from the area. Caleb Donahue was last seen just one day after Alice disappeared. For more on this case and what police are asking of the community, we go on location to Sherwood and Sheriff Samuel Johnson."

My breath catches in my chest, and I slowly lower down to sit on the couch. The image on the screen shifts to a podium perched in front of a large crowd of onlookers and reporters. Several police officers stand to either side of the podium, and in a few seconds, another man steps up behind it. He's wearing a sheriff's uniform and a drawn, exhausted look on his face.

"Thank you for joining us this afternoon. As of today, Alice Brooks has been missing for two weeks. Camp has continued on as planned in hopes Alice will return, or someone will notice something that leads us to her. The search for her has become even more urgent, as we've recently become aware of another missing child. Caleb Donahue just turned eleven three days before his disappearance. He has a very large extended family and frequently spends time with both of his parents, and his aunts and uncles, as well as his adult siblings. An unfortunate miscommunication left the various members of the family believing Caleb was with different people. He was thought to have joined different groups of his family for trips, as he commonly did during breaks from school. It was not until his mother made contact with Caleb's father to remind him of an upcoming dental appointment that she discovered he was not where she believed him to be."

He flips the page of his notes and rubs his mouth.

"Both parents reached out to the family, as well as friends throughout the area, but no one knew where Caleb was and had not heard from him since the day he left a sleepover at a friend's house to return home. Though there is little to go on with either case, the similarities between the disappearances have led us to believe the two may be related. We're asking for the community's help finding these children and bringing them home safely. If you know anything about either child, have seen anything suspicious, or have any information you think may be helpful, please do not hesitate to call the department. A hotline has been set up specifically for this case. Keep in mind that even a small detail may be the exact bit of information we need. Alice Brooks is ten years old, white, with dark blond hair and green eyes. She is four feet, eight inches tall, and weighs seventy-eight pounds. Caleb Donahue is eleven years old, black, with short black hair and brown eyes. He is five feet tall and weighs eighty-three pounds. Right now, we are considering both children in serious danger."

The sheriff waves off questions from the rapid reporters gathered around the stage and steps away from the podium. A second later, the image flashes back to the newscaster. She makes the kind of generically sympathetic and concerned statement that wraps up the story and acts as a transition to the next, but I don't hear what it is. I can't pull myself out of the statement I just heard. One child missing could be a fluke, a little girl who walked away from camp and got lost. Two children missing from the same small town so close together is something much more. It can't be a coincidence. The fear and concern in his eyes are justified.

I haven't shaken the feeling of watching Sheriff Johnson make that pleading statement the next day as I make all the last-minute preparations for leaving. He was doing everything he could to sound strong and be the leader of his community. He knew everyone was looking to him for guidance and reassurance. Even if he didn't have the right words to say or the answers to give them, he would show them he could be steady during the tumultuous time. I know that very well.

I'm expecting Bellamy's call when my phone rings. She's supposed to be coming over for dinner to see me off, which means she's going to go through at least four different ideas for what she's going to pick up. The times in our friendship when she has an idea of what to grab for dinner and that actually being what she ends up with by the time we got together have been very few and far between.

"Yes, Bellamy?" I answer.

"I'm torn between Indian food and Thai. Curry sounds so good right now. But so does rama," she tells me.

"Thai."

"Okay. I'll be there soon."

I hang up and start my tour around the house to check all the entrance points the police identified for me. They gave me a list and made me promise to go through and specifically check each one of them twice before leaving. Once today and once just before Eric takes me to the airport. They even suggested I place bits of tape or small objects on the windowsills so I can quickly tell if someone came into the house and how they got in.

I understand the sentiment behind it, but it seems unduly complicated. Besides, if this person is going through the effort of slipping into my home so I can't tell, I highly doubt a strip of tape or sugar scattered on the windowsill is going to go unnoticed. They could just as easily figure out a way to put it back into place. I tell myself at least it would be another hint, another clue as to what is going on. If we can figure out where they were getting into the house, it will make it easier to create more effective surveillance.

My phone rings in the bedroom when I'm in the spare room. I don't mind the excuse to get out of the room as fast as I can. This is his space and holds a desk, swivel chair, and bookshelves brimming with true crime books and case files. Even though this room hasn't been used in years, I can feel my father in it.

Confident the windows in the room are secure, I close the door and hurry back into my bedroom. I sweep my phone off the bed and hold it between my shoulder and ear so I can answer while folding the laundry still sitting in a basket from the loads I washed this morning.

"As long as it isn't fried chicken and doesn't come from a convenience store, I'm fine with it," I offer. "Actually, maybe fried chicken."

"That sounds delicious, but looking for dinner plans isn't why I'm calling you."

The man's voice isn't what I expected to come through the line. My phone nearly slips from my grasp. I grab it with my hand and sit on the edge of my bed.

"Why are you calling me?" I ask.

"This is…"

"I know who it is," I say, stopping him. "I saw your press conference on the news last night."

The sheriff draws in a slight breath.

"Then that saves me the effort of explaining what's going on," he sighs. "You must know why I'm calling."

"What do you mean?"

"I need your help."

Air I didn't realize I was holding rushes out of me.

"Why do you need my help?"

"There are no clues. No leads. Nothing. An entire community is terrified, and they're looking to me to figure this out for them, but I don't have anything to tell them. I've never dealt with anything like this before, and I don't have any idea what to do next."

"The Bureau hasn't gotten involved in the investigation as far as I know. And if it has, I'm not part of the team assigned to it."

"The FBI hasn't been brought in. I'm not calling them for help. I'm calling you, specifically," he says.

I get up from the bed and go back to folding the blanket in my hands to stop my mind from following that sentiment too far.

"I'm leaving for vacation tomorrow morning. I'll be away for a week, then I'll have a few days before I go back to work," I tell the sheriff.

"That's too long," he says.

"I'm sorry. My flight leaves at ten tomorrow, and I'll be back …"

"Emma, another child is gone."

CHAPTER ELEVEN

The morning sunlight barely making it through the clouds promises a gloomy day. Overcast and gray, the sky has captured all the humidity and heat, pressing it down until it creates an oppressive, wet feeling in the air. I've heard the summertime weather in Virginia described in many different ways, but the one that's probably the most accurate is that it feels like living in a rice steamer. Constantly hot and wet, the only release coming with the thunderstorms and the occasional floral scented breeze that breaks the stillness at night.

"Call me if you change your mind," Eric says. "I'll come back and get you anytime."

"I know you will, thank you," I say.

"You're absolutely sure of this?" he asks.

I look through the windshield at the gathering storm.

"Yes. I'm already on my way. It's going to be fine. I know it is."

"And if it's not?" Eric asks. "If you get there and everything else takes a major turn?"

"Then I figure it out. But for right now, this is what I need to do," I tell him.

"Just be careful and if you need me, call me," he says. "I can be to you in less than two hours."

"I know. You've done it before. And I promise I'll be careful."

I press the end call button on my phone, where it's attached to a stand on my dash. This isn't how today was supposed to go. An hour from now, Eric is supposed to pick me up to take me to the airport so I can go on my much-needed vacation. Instead, he's back in his apartment, and I'm on a lonely stretch of road on my way to the past.

As soon as I got off the phone with Sheriff Johnson last night, I knew there was no way I'd be able to go on my trip the way I planned. The thought of a third missing child gnawed on the back of my mind and made my stomach turn. One missing child is painful. Two missing children is a serious situation. Three missing children is a serial kidnapper. I've done this long enough to know that once a person hits the designation of being serial, whether it's a killer, kidnapper, or a rapist, they're unlikely to just stop. There's a reason they collect as many victims as they do, and it's not because they're there. A serial criminal has a compulsion, and they have to follow it. It's like their breath, their heartbeat, a primal element of themselves that pushes them forward.

Not every one of them is out of control. Most people would like to think that one human being who is capable of the torment, torture, and even murder of another human being, much less several of them, must have an inherent flaw. They want them to be irreconcilably mentally ill, or fundamentally damaged in a way that distinctly and readily identifiably separates them from other people. The reality is that's not usually the case. There will always be the ones who are abnormal and suffering from trauma or illness that lead to their crimes. But the existence of those people doesn't eliminate the reality of the others who commit their crimes purely out of their own desires. There's a driving force, a motivation so appealing and offering so many rewards; it's hard to resist.

That's where the real fear begins. If there's truly a serial kidnapper in Sherwood, it's only a matter of time before another child is taken. Three in a matter of weeks is gut-wrenching frequency. The goal now must be not just to find the three children whose mothers are aching to hold them again, but to stop the next from disappearing.

Getting a phone call from Johnson was startling, and instantly, my reluctance to going back to Sherwood disappeared. It's been a long time since I was there. So many years since I laid eyes on the town I for all intents and purposes consider my home.

The concept of home means different things to different people. For some, it's wherever their family is. For others, it's where they were born and raised. And for yet more, it's wherever they happen to live at that time and is redefined as easily as they pack up their belongings and choose another house. I've struggled throughout my life with what I see as my home.

In a lot of ways, I never really had one. But Sherwood was always there. I was home if I was with my parents, but the physical location we lived at changed so often I sometimes forgot where I was. If my parents ever talked about where we were living at any given time, they would say 'the house' or 'our place'.

If they ever talked about going 'home', I knew they meant we were going back to the quiet town where my father grew up. We were going back to the tree-lined streets and family-owned businesses. Yards dotted with flowers or blanketed with the type of color-saturated foliage people flock to drive past each fall. Jewel-toned leaves that families leaned out of car windows to ogle at. That packed picnics so they could sit among them and absorb as much of their beauty as they could. That filled children's hands and became piles to jump in.

That was Sherwood as I grew up, barely changing between the stretches when we lived there. We went back several times throughout my childhood and teen years. My grandparents' house features in many of the memories I have of holidays, studying for tests, and feeling normal. I would stretch out on the couch my grandmother draped with a crisp, cool sheet brought fresh out of her linen closet just for me. There were times I lay on that couch, thinking we were done running. I thought maybe this was the beginning of a normal life.

But it never happened that way. Soon enough, all our belongings, or as much as we could gather together in the time we had, were shoved into the car, and we were on our way again. Every time we left, my grandparents stood out in the front yard, their arms around each other's waists, smiling and waving goodbye. They never looked afraid or uncertain. It was like we were simply going for a weekend away. But I always left with a rock in the pit of my stomach, wondering if that was the last time we were going to leave Sherwood.

Last time I did, it was on my own terms. I didn't think I would ever go back. Even this morning, as I got behind the wheel of my car and started in the direction of my hometown, it didn't feel real. But I can't pretend it's not now.

The green and cream-colored paint on the sign welcoming me into town looks the exact same as it did when I put it behind me eleven years ago. I'm sure it's been touched up during that time, but the wear and cracks are in the same places, and I feel like if I look closely enough, I'll find the thumbprint I pressed into the back corner when the edge was still damp.

Reminders of everything I left behind rise up on either side of me as my car slows to match the rhythm of life here. If I close my eyes, I can still follow the right path. I'll end up right in the driveway, flanked by pink azalea bushes, facing the slab of concrete left in the ground after my grandfather finally took down the old above ground pool.

It looks like a postcard and sounds like the soundtrack of a vintage summer. But maybe quieter now. Less laughter. Fewer children splashing in pools and running through sprinklers. Parents whispering rather than talking over sweating glasses of iced tea.

The farther I drive into town, the more my heart aches. Some of it is for the missing children and the fear that swallowed the joy of July days. But I know more is from pain along the fault lines, from cracks that never fully healed. Some shards aren't there anymore. They're here. Those pieces of my broken heart are among the many things I left behind when I left Sherwood, never intending to come back.

I drive past the high school, where a graduation balloon sags helplessly from the end of the fence. I should have graduated there, walked across the stage with the classmates whose lives I drifted in and out of but managed to find space for me. Instead, a tutor accelerated me through Junior and Senior year together, so I finished a year early and graduated with an email and a brisk note of congratulations sent along with my diploma. By the time my friends here were tossing their hats in the air, I was in college. Most of my friends. Some took that leap out of childhood even before me.

I didn't leave early enough to stop anywhere before getting to the station. By the time I pull into a parking space and walk into the bracing air conditioning of the lobby, the clock ticks onto eight.

"Exactly on time. Like always."

The voice is somehow deeper when it's not coming through the phone. I turn around and see the tall, dark-haired man from behind the podium at the press conference sitting in a chair in the waiting area.

"Sam," I say.

He stands up, and as he takes a step toward me, I can see the broken pieces I left behind in his eyes.

"Emma, thank you for coming."

CHAPTER TWELVE

The waitress at the coffee shop on the corner looks familiar. She already has two mugs down and a stream of hot, powerful coffee filling the one in front of Sam by the time I've settled into place on my side of the booth. I look into her round face, tinted with pink from heat and the exertion of the morning rush. It takes a few seconds for me to realize it's the same woman who brought me coffee and a slab of country ham on a biscuit the morning I said goodbye to Sherwood. She's older and softer, but her smile hasn't wavered. She still looks happy to be here, like she's welcoming friends to her own kitchen table rather than waiting tables at a coffee shop that's served several generations before her.

"Thank you, Molly," Sam says.

"Absolutely, Sheriff. Will you be having your regular this morning?"

"Yes, that'll be fine. Emma here might need a menu, though. It's been a little while since she's ordered breakfast here."

It's a hidden message, a hint to her to confirm my face is the one she thinks she's looking at. I know it's changed far more than hers has. While she fits in here as if she's as much a part of the space as the checkerboard floor and smooth Formica tabletops, I'm an anomaly.

"Emma Griffin, I thought that was you," Molly smiles. "I never thought I'd see the day when you'd come back here."

"Stranger things have happened," I shrug. "It's nice to see you."

"Nice to see you, too. Is your daddy with you?"

I draw in a breath and swallow it down with a swig of coffee. I can feel Sam's eyes on me and know his mind is churning, wondering what I'm going to say. I flash the waitress a smile.

"I'll have two eggs sunny-side up and a biscuit. Thank you," I tell her.

She looks at me strangely but doesn't let her smile fade.

"Coming right up," she says.

Sam reaches for the tiny pitcher of cream sitting at the edge of the table and swirls it into his coffee. Two packets of sugar shake between his fingers and tumble into the mug. I know those movements like I know my own. I've seen them so many times before. Some right here in this shop. Many more times at other tables, in other worlds, in other lives.

"It sure is hot this summer," he says, falling into the age-old routine of small talk.

He's wading into the shallows before braving the deeper water. Like he fears the current that might take him.

"It always is," I reply.

He takes a sip of his coffee and adds the third packet of sugar he might as well put in with the first two because it always follows.

"I suppose that's true. Just feels hotter than I remember it. Maybe because I'm wearing this uniform now. It's not exactly as breathable as when I used to wear nothing but shorts or a bathing suit in the summertime."

Images of those days conjure in my mind before I can do anything to stop them. Some are when he was young, little more than beanpole arms and the hope of chest muscles as he ran around with his younger sisters and did his best to drain the community pool with cannonballs. That hope was fulfilled the next time I came back to Sherwood, but the smile across the pool was still all boy. His hair hung down over his eyes, and his bathing suit slung low over his hips. Later there would

74

be a deep V of muscle there, and my fingertips traced them like I was tracing his evolution.

"Not as many chances to do that when you're an adult," I tell him.

He nods as if I've given him some sage advice, then pauses as his deep emerald eyes follow the lines of my face and settle on the pulse at the base of my throat before rising up again.

"Are you staying up at the hotel?" he asks.

The question hits me hard for some reason, and I hesitate a few seconds before shaking my head.

"Um, no. My grandparents' house has been vacant for a couple months since the couple renting it moved out to California. I contacted the management company that's been overseeing it and told them I'd be staying in it for a few days while I'm here. It'll be a good chance to check it over and make sure it's still in good condition. They send me pictures, and maintenance reports twice a year, but it hasn't been empty for a long time, and I want to see if anything major needs to be done before somebody else moves in," I explain.

"Have you been there yet?"

"No. I came straight to the station. I'll go over there when we're done here."

He lets out a long breath.

"You look good, Emma," he says.

My hands tighten around the mug. I can't do this. Not this. Not now.

"Sam, I didn't stop in for breakfast with you because I was passing through. I'm here because you called me to ask for help. Let's just skip by the Hallmark reunion and get to the point."

Molly appears at the side of the table and looks between us awkwardly as she lowers the plates she's carrying in each hand down to the table.

"Can I get anything else for you?" she asks.

We both shake our heads, and she walks away. I wait until she's engrossed in gossip and refilling a coffee mug across the shop to lean slightly toward Sam.

"How did you get my phone number, anyway?" I whisper.

"I contacted the alumni association," he tells me.

He picks up his knife and starts smearing softened butter on a piece of toast. I shake my head.

"My number isn't listed in the directory."

"No, but they have it from when you did that talk on young women in law enforcement a couple of years ago."

"And they just gave it to you when you said you wanted it?" I ask.

"I told them who I was and that it was important."

I sigh and pick up my fork to stab the yolk of one of my eggs. It oozes perfectly across the whites and puddles up near the butter-crisped edge.

"Well, I'm so glad they got so many valuable takeaways from my section on cyber safety and identity protection," I mutter.

"I wouldn't have had to do that if you didn't make it impossible to find you," he points out.

"It's not impossible to find me. I just don't make it so just anyone can get to me whenever they want to."

Thoughts of the envelope and the necklace flash through my mind, and I shake them off.

"I didn't realize I was just anyone," he protests. "And it isn't like I did it for no reason."

"Sam, that's not what I meant."

"Remember, Emma; you're the one who walked away. That wasn't my decision."

I close my eyes and hold my hands out to stop him.

"Stop. This isn't why I'm here. I'm here because you asked for my help. Even though I'm still not certain why you did that," I say.

"Because you're the only person who I can think of who might have the insight we need to solve this. I don't want any other children disappearing, Emma. Three is far too many as it is. We've been investigating and doing everything we can around the clock since we got the call about Alice Brooks, and we've gotten nowhere. We are no further along in finding her or figuring out who took her, then we were that first night. And now two other children are missing. Asking for help isn't something I like doing. Trust me; if I didn't feel like this

THE GIRL THAT VANISHED

was the only way, I never would have done it. But you know Sherwood. You know this place and its people. You know one of the families involved. And you have the skills from the Bureau to maybe see this in a way we can't."

"What do you mean I know one of the families involved?" I ask.

"The third child went missing yesterday morning. A little ten-year-old girl named Eva Francis."

"Francis? As in Francis, the family who lived across the street from my grandparents?"

He nods.

"They still live there. Eva is their granddaughter. They have been raising her since she was just a few months old. Their son hooked up with some girl and got her pregnant after knowing her for just a few weeks. As soon as the baby was born, she left town. They only hear from her a few times a year when she sends a little bit of money and asks for pictures. Jimmy was by all accounts excited to be a father, but you can only straighten out a wire coat hanger but so much. Part of it's bound to stay crooked. A few months after Eva was born, he got caught up with the wrong guys, decided to try to make some fast money, and landed an eight-year sentence. While he was in, he jumped a couple of other guys to prove his place in the hierarchy and ended up tacking on another five. He and Eva were already living with his parents, so they just took her on like she was their own. Raised her to be nothing like her parents. Now she's gone." He leans closer and drops his voice. "I need you, Emma. Please, say you'll help me."

A bright light flashing in my eyes stops me before I can answer him. My head snaps to the window, where a man in jeans and a button-down shirt rolled at his elbows takes another picture. He lifts his hand to his mouth and seems to mutter something like he's recording what he's saying.

"Who the hell is that?" I ask as Sam stands up sharply and stalks out of the coffee shop.

I rush to follow him, watching him step up close to the man, who stands his ground, not seeming bothered by Sam's approach.

"Get out of here, William," he growls. "I told you to stop sniffing around here. You come to the press conferences and nothing else."

"Freedom of the press, Sam," the man fires back with an expression I can only describe as a smirk.

"That's Sheriff Johnson to you," Sam tells him. "And you'll do as I say, or I'll bring you in for harassment and impeding an investigation."

"Sheriff, I am not on your private property. I'm not bothering you in your home. I'm standing on a public sidewalk."

"Taking a picture of me through a coffee shop window," Sam points out.

I stride up to the two men and look the man in the eye.

"What's going on here?" I ask.

"Emma, this is William Jennings, a pain in my ass."

"You flatter me," Jennings says, then turns his attention to me. "I'm actually a reporter."

"I gathered that." I narrow my eyes at him.

Jennings eyes me, and I notice a red light in his palm that tells me he's recording the entire interaction.

"So, Sheriff, do you frequently include breakfast dates in your investigations? Are taxpayer dollars paying for this cozy little meeting?" he asks.

"This isn't a date," I tell him bluntly.

"And as a matter of fact, this is part of the investigation," Sam tells him. "This is Emma Griffin. She's with the FBI."

I cringe internally at the same moment Jennings's lips coil up like the Grinch's.

"Oh, really?" he asks.

"I am not officially involved in the investigation, and neither is the Bureau," I tell him. "I'm here in a consulting capacity because of my personal knowledge of the town."

The reporter smiles and slips his phone into his pocket.

"Have a good day, Ms. Griffin. Sheriff," he says, ducking into a black car parked nearby.

"Well, shit," I murmur.

CHAPTER THIRTEEN

"I s something wrong?" Sam asks. "Was I not supposed to mention you're with the Bureau?"

I shake my head, rubbing my eyes.

"No. I mean, it's not a secret. I'm not a covert agent, and I'll just be sure to avoid this general area if I have to go undercover again at any point. It's right there on my business card."

"Then what's the problem?"

"I told you when you called me. I'm supposed to be on vacation right now," I say, heading back into the coffee shop to finish eating. "And I didn't exactly tell my boss about the change of plans."

"I don't understand. Aren't you allowed to do whatever you want with your vacation time?"

"Not when taking that vacation time off comes along with a thera-pist recommendation," I tell him.

While my therapist wasn't thrilled at the idea of me bounding off to Iowa when I told her about it, she has been a strong supporter of me taking a couple of weeks off and wasn't shy about telling Creagan that.

"What do you mean?" Sam asks.

"Never mind. I really don't want to get into it right now. Tell me who that guy was."

"I did. That's William Jennings."

"I got that. And I got that he's a reporter. But what's with him lurking around outside restaurant windows and you acting like you're ready to pick him up and throw him through said window?"

Sam shoves a forkful of toast layered with scrambled eggs and bacon into his mouth and shakes his head.

"Jennings is from around here. You probably don't remember him. He was a couple of years in front of me in school. Always thought he was destined for bigger and better things than Sherwood. He was big into the newspaper at the high school and interned for the local paper around here. Then he started doing little spots on the local news and eventually went off to college to study mass communication. But he ended up back here. That only lasted a couple of years before he moved into the city to chase being an investigative reporter. He's made a pretty good name for himself, but it's not enough for him. He wants to be bigger. More famous. More money."

"All the glitz and glamor of death and turmoil," I comment.

"Essentially."

"Now that you tell me that, I think I have heard his name before. He's covered a few bigger stories," I say.

Sam nods. "Middle ground stuff. But if you ask him, it's just a ramp to the big time. He's going to get his claws in a story that rocks the country and launches him into being a household name."

"And you think he's angling to make this that story?"

"Been trying hard to keep media involvement to an absolute minimum. These families are already going through enough. They don't need cameras in their faces and strangers screaming at them and vying for sound bites. This is a tragedy for them. The worst time in their lives. It isn't something they can just wrap up into a neat little statement that sounds sexy on the six o'clock news. But that's what Jennings is trying to make out of it. Other reporters and news stations have had the decency to respect our boundaries and stick to the press conferences and pre-arranged interviews. Not him. He takes freedom of press very seriously."

"Why does he care where you're having breakfast?" I ask.

"Nothing makes a news story as gut-wrenching as three children disappearing more compelling than being able to say the sheriff in charge isn't doing everything he can to solve the case. He wants to make me out to be a failure in my post." Sam hangs his head. "Not that I don't already feel that way."

"Sam, you are not a failure. I watched you on that press conference. I know how much this means to you and how hard you've been working to find these children. Anyone who looks at you can see it in your eyes."

"I think you can probably see it more," he says quietly.

I look down at my plate, so I don't have to look at him. He's behind me. I put him there a long time ago, and I did it on purpose. I'm not here to put him in front of me again.

"What's happening in the investigation today?" I ask, shifting our conversation back to the path where it's supposed to be.

"The team is going to spend some time talking with the families of the two more recently missing children. Then we're going to plan how to release information about Eva's disappearance. As of right now, you are the only person outside of the investigation who knows about it. We are trying to find a way to inform the community without causing panic. At this point, we also want to start being more selective about the information we release so we can identify suspects if they cross our paths."

"How does the rest of the department feel about my involvement?" I ask.

"They don't know," he admits. "I didn't know if you were going to be willing to help or how much, so I didn't tell them."

"Well, I suggest you make a phone call because as soon as Jennings gets to a computer, it's not going to be a secret anymore. Dangling an FBI agent as a part of child disappearances in front of a thirsty reporter is like candy. He's going to trot it out in front of anybody he can, to get his foot in as many doors as possible, then start collecting bids. You don't want the rest of the department finding out that way," I tell him.

"Are you saying you'll help?" he asks.

"As long as you understand I'm not here in any official capacity as an agent. I can consult and act as a sounding board, but the Bureau isn't involved."

"I understand that."

"We shouldn't talk here," I say, as more people start drifting in. "Do what you need to do today, and I'll get settled. If you're available later, you can give me any information you can, and we'll get to work."

"I don't know when I'll be able to leave the station, but I can let you know, and we can meet somewhere."

"That's fine with me," I nod.

"Thank you, Emma."

We finish eating in silence. I'm not sure if it's the comfortable kind of two people who have known each other for most of their lives, or the unavoidable kind that comes from years of separation and the unspoken words that want their place.

When we get back to the station, we part ways outside the door with only a cursory nod and reconfirmation of our plans for later in the day. My car is sticky hot when I get inside. It reminds me of driving through town with my grandmother when I was a little girl. She had a long navy-blue Pontiac with leather seats and the 1970's version of air conditioning. Which meant the windows rolled down from the first day of spring weather until September. Sometimes later depending on the year.

The inside of that car got so hot it was like climbing into a furnace. My skin stuck to the seats, and the metal seatbelt buckles burned my thighs. During the hottest part of summer, she would drape the seats with towels, making sure the seatbelts were covered. It kept the sun off the gleaming metal so I could actually touch it when I got inside.

My air conditioner is thankfully contemporary, and by the time I turn into the grocery store parking lot, the refrigerant is pumping blissfully cold air across my face. I'm reluctant to turn the car off, but the house has nothing in it, and if I'm going to be there longer than today, I'll need supplies.

Half an hour later, I'm sitting in the driveway, flanked by pink azaleas, staring at the concrete that used to hold the above ground pool. My father declared the pool no longer usable and dragged it away the summer I turned seventeen when duct tape and nostalgia couldn't hold it up anymore.

I lift my eyes to the rearview mirror and see the buttery yellow house with blue shutters across the street. Janet and Paul Francis were a vibrant, energetic couple in their late thirties the last time I saw them. My grandparents had a much more open attitude toward neighbors than I do, and my grandmother had a fondness for the younger woman who shared her love of flowers and the tendency to drown them.

The result was both lawns boasting planters that bloomed gloriously for a few weeks and ended up empty by mid-summer. I didn't spend a lot of time with the Francis's in the times I was here, but I remember them enough to feel a hollow feeling in my chest looking at their house, thinking of a sweetly decorated bedroom with no little girl to tuck into bed.

I also remember their son. A brooding, impulsive boy who could be pleasant one minute and then fly into a rage the next. Hearing his little daughter brought a bright spot into his life was nice, but I never had any doubt he would end up exactly where he is.

I've stalled long enough. No matter how strong my air conditioner is, my ice cream is melting in the backseat. Gathering the bags, I pluck the key I picked up from the management company on the way to the house out of the cupholder and head for the front door.

The lock is smooth, and the door swings open, revealing the polished wood floor of the entryway beyond. My father arranged for the house to be rented out by the management company fully furnished, so when I glance into the rooms on either side of me, they look like someone has just walked out of them and will be back at any second. I close the door behind me and step into the quiet.

I'm home.

CHAPTER FOURTEEN

He's holding fried chicken.

I have to blink a few times to make sure I'm actually seeing what my eyes tell me I am.

Sam is standing on my front porch, holding fried chicken.

He lowers the hand holding the bulging white bag I'm sure also has a box of biscuits and containers of mashed potatoes and coleslaw and lifts the other. It's holding a jug of sweet tea.

"I didn't have time to make any, and I figured you didn't have a jar of your Granny's sun tea sitting on the back porch," he explains.

"I certainly hope I don't," I say. "That would be some severely over-brewed tea."

The memory of my grandmother filling a big mason jar with water and tea bags and setting it out in the sun makes my heart warm. But it also brings me sharply and aggressively back to Feathered Nest and my hand sliding over a quilt. I told Jake I didn't get to spend much time with my grandparents when I was younger. That my memories of them were scattered and brief. It feels like that sometimes. Like everyone else has continuous memories of seeing their grandparents every Sunday for dinner or spending days with them a few times a month. I don't have that. There are swaths of time, sometimes years-long, when I didn't see them at all. That makes me feel like I didn't get to spend time with them or that I don't have as many memories of them as I should.

But right now, I realize that isn't really true. Sure, there are times in my life when I didn't get to spend time with them. There are things I wish I got to share with them and moments I feel they should have been a part of. But there are also stretches of time I got to immerse myself in them. The memory of the quilt folded over the back of the couch is from a long winter we settled in and didn't leave. That quilt surrounded me when I was a baby. It gave me comfort when I was a little girl and caught chickenpox. It was still there when we finally came back.

"Emma? Are you alright?"

I come back into reality and see Sam staring at me with a concerned expression on his face.

"Yeah. I was just… nothing. Come on in." I step out of the way and let him walk past me. "Fried chicken. I see what you did there. Cute."

He shrugs. "I've been thinking about it since you mentioned it to me the other day."

"Well, I didn't actually mention it to you. I thought I was talking to someone else," I say.

I gesture for him to go into the living room. It feels strange to have him here in the house, but it was the only logical place for us to meet. Anywhere else had the risk of someone hearing us discuss the sensitive details of the case. He puts the bag of food down on the coffee table, and I go into the kitchen to get plates and glasses.

"Your boyfriend?" he asks.

"What?" I ask, coming back into the room.

"Your boyfriend," he repeats. "Did you think you were mentioning the fried chicken to him?"

My throat feels slightly dry as I pop the top on the jug of sweet tea and pour some into the glasses.

"No," I shake my head. "My friend Bellamy."

"From college?" he asks. "The two of you are still close?"

"I actually knew her before college. Not for long, but I met her when I was younger. We kind of kept in touch, and then realized we were both going to the same college."

"I didn't realize that," Sam says. "I thought you met there. You never told me you knew her before. I guess reuniting with you at college is something she and I have in common."

Handing him one of the glasses, I nod. "I guess you do."

A few tense seconds pass, and he climbs to his feet, giving me a second to breathe.

"I'll be right back," he says, heading back out of the house. He returns moments later, holding a cardboard box with a leather satchel sitting on top. He sits it down on the floor beside the table. "Case notes."

"The leather is very classy," I note.

He shoots me a look and yanks papers out of the satchel, setting them on the box and putting the bag on the floor.

"It was a graduation gift from my father," he says.

His phone buzzes at the same time mine starts ringing. I cringe at the name on the screen and walk away from the table to answer it.

"Hi, Creagan," I sigh.

"What do I need to do to get through to you?"

That is not a happy voice.

Sam walks up to me and shows me his phone. The picture Jennings took is even more unflattering than I thought it was going to be, but it's the headline that really stands out.

"Alright. Let me explain what's going on," I say.

"I went to work this morning feeling pretty optimistic. After all the shit you've been through, I was seriously starting to worry about you. But you were finally going to take some time off, try to relieve some stress. I spent all day thinking you were off baking yourself on the beach."

"That was the plan…"

"And then I scroll through the news and what do I see? You're not on a beach. You're in Virginia. Eating breakfast."

The conversation doesn't get much better. By the time I stop my rambling tour of the house and get back to the living room, Sam is pouring his second glass of tea and reaching for another biscuit.

"Well," I say, kneeling down on the floor beside the table. "That was my boss. He read the same article."

"How did he take it?" Sam asks.

"We'll go with not delighted. But willing to let me help."

"I'm sorry if I caused you any trouble."

"I was going to piss him off again eventually. If we can find these kids, it's worth it. Let's get started," I say.

I dish out a plate of food, and the first taste of the diner's chicken is like being sixteen again. Sitting on the grass by the lake at the edge of town, eating a picnic of cold fried chicken and coleslaw while Fourth of July fireworks burst overhead. I get a few more bites in, but soon the food is forgotten as Sam and I delve deep into the details of the case.

"There are a few similarities between the children and their disappearances," he points out. "They are within a year of each other in age. They are all local children, not visitors. And they all disappeared while doing something outside of their regular routine."

"What do you mean?" I ask.

"Alice Brooks was at summer camp for the first time. Caleb Donahue was at a slumber party with a friend he'd never slept over with before. He was supposed to walk home, but where he was supposed to go or who he was supposed to be with after that gets fuzzy. Eva Francis was supposed to be going to a water park with her church group but wasn't at the house when the van got there to pick her up."

"Where were her grandparents?" I ask.

"They left for work less than twenty minutes before the van arrived. According to them, she is not left alone normally, but because she was going to be gone all day and then was attending the lock-in at the church planned for after the trip, they decided to both work that day. They thought she would be safe at home for such a short period of time."

"Anything else? Families who work in the same places? Same hobbies? Babysitters?" I ask.

"No. They all attend the elementary school, but that's it. Two of them are girls. One boy. Alice is white. Caleb is black. Eva is white and Hispanic. They have different family arrangements. Different faiths. All the threads that usually link serial kidnapping victims... they just aren't there."

I spread out pictures of the three children and look at them, trying to figure out what could link them. There has to be something. Truly random victims are incredibly rare. Most of the time, criminals have something specific that leads them to choose the specific individuals they do. Sometimes it's as simple as them being in a certain place when the perpetrator wants to strike. But these children were taken from different places in different circumstances. It wasn't just a matter of convenience. Suddenly my eyes are drawn to the names scribbled under the images. I read through them several times, then adjust the position of the pictures, so they are in order of when they disappeared.

"Did you notice this?" I ask, pointing at the names.

He follows my finger, and his eyes widen. "It's a pattern."

I nod. "Alice Brooks. A, B. Caleb Donahue. C, D. Eva Francis. E, F. Their names are going in alphabetical order by first and last name."

Bolstered by the tiny step forward, we dig through every piece of evidence and detail in the case files until I notice Sam's eyes drooping.

"Have you been getting any sleep?" I ask.

"Some," he says.

"Does 'some' mean you occasionally put your head down on your desk?" I ask.

"I've stretched out on the couch in my office a couple of times," he nods.

"When we were in college, I watched you study for three days with no more than two hours of sleep. I supplied you with coffee to get you through some of it. And this is much more serious than Advanced

Chemistry. You have to sleep. You aren't going to be any good to anyone if you exhaust yourself."

I'm lecturing even as the burn of my eyes reminds me of the hours I've lost.

"Let me go crash, and I'll call you in the morning," he says.

"Good idea." I follow him to the door. "Thanks for the fried chicken."

He smiles, and I'm torn down the middle. Part of me wakes up with that smile and part of me recoils.

"Any time. Good night, Emma."

"Good night."

I close the door behind him and clean up the remnants of dinner before heading into the bedroom I slept in when I was younger. It doesn't look the same, but it feels just as it did. I change into pajamas and slip into the cool sheets, wondering if my nightmares can find me here.

CHAPTER FIFTEEN

The next morning comes early. I feel like the sharp ringing of my phone under my pillow snaps me out of sleep almost as soon as I finally find it. First, it seems like the sun hasn't even come up yet, but then I realize it's just another densely clouded morning. Glancing at the clock at the side of the bed, I see it's past dawn, but just barely. I pull myself up to sitting and run my fingers back through my hair to get it out of my eyes, then reach around for my phone without looking.

"Hello?"

"Emma, get dressed. I'll be there to pick you up in ten minutes," Sam says.

That opens my eyes the rest of the way but puts a sinking feeling in my stomach.

"What's going on?" I asked.

"A reporter thinks he has information about Alice Brooks."

"A reporter? Are you talking about Jennings?"

"No. This is another local reporter. He got in touch with me about twenty minutes ago and apparently has something he needs to show me. He seems really worked up about it," Sam tells me.

"I'll be ready," I say.

Questions and possibilities twist and turn through my mind as I throw on a pair of jeans and a black tank top. I pull my hair back into a ponytail and swipe on a couple of coats of mascara to make me look more awake. I've just finished putting my shoes on when Sam pulls up in front of the house. I climb in the passenger seat, and he offers a travel cup of coffee.

"Cream and sugar," he says.

"Thank you," I nod. "So, what's going on? What is this reporter talking about?"

"I'm not sure yet. He says he wants to show me."

"And you trust this guy? I mean, you know who he is?"

"I know him. Vincent Lam. He's not like Jennings. He's never had the chance to be," he says.

We drive to the other side of town into a modest neighborhood and park in front of a meticulously kept brick house. The engine isn't even off when a man appears at the screen door. He waits there as we walk up the sidewalk, and I notice his eyes lock on me.

"Good morning, Vincent," Sam says.

"Morning, Sheriff. I was hoping to be able to speak only to you about this."

I have to give him credit. He's straightforward. Not beating around the bush saves a lot of time.

"It's alright, Vincent," Sam reassures him. "This is Emma Griffin. She's helping me with the investigation."

The sandy haired man scrutinizes me for a few seconds before he finally nods.

"Alright," he says. "Come in."

We follow him inside, and he leads us into a small office taking up the front corner of the house. Several pieces of paper spread out across a desk catch my eye. I walk up to the desk and look down at the papers.

"This is what you got?" I ask.

Vincent nods and walks up to the other side of the desk.

"I went out to get the paper this morning, and there was a big manila envelope on the porch. I opened it, and these were inside," he explains.

"Was there anything written on the outside of the envelope?" Sam asks.

"Just my last name," he says.

"Can I see it?" I ask.

Vincent reaches under the papers and pulls out a standard-sized manila envelope. He slides it across the desk toward me, and I look at the name. Written in basic block print in black permanent marker, it's anonymous enough that nearly anyone could have written it. I peek inside, but there's nothing else.

"These are the two that makes me think this has something to do with the first girl," Vincent says.

He points out two of the papers, and Sam and I look at them. The first depicts the little blond girl in a blue dress seeming to tumble down from the sky. There is nothing else in the picture, no surroundings or objects, but it's instantly recognizable.

"Alice," I say. "Like Alice in Wonderland."

Vincent nods and points to the other paper, which has a simplified pencil sketch of running water stretched diagonally across it.

"Brook. The little girl's last name is Brooks, but that's close."

"It is," Sam nods. "What about the other papers?"

The reporter reaches for another stack of papers, and I hear a door slam behind us.

"What's going on here?" a woman asks as she comes into the room.

She looks distinctly unhappy to see us standing there.

"Honey, I told you I was going to call the sheriff about this," Vincent says.

"Emma, this is Valerie," Sam says.

"I'm Vincent's wife," the woman tells me forcefully, stepping up beside her husband and taking his hand.

"Hello," I say, reaching out my hand toward her. "I'm Emma Griffin. I..."

"I know who you are," she interrupts coldly. "What I want to know is what interest the FBI has in my husband."

"As far as I know, there's no reason for the Bureau to have any interest in your husband at all. I'm acting as a consultant for Sheriff Johnson. Your husband is the one who called us," I tell her.

As if she didn't register what Vincent said to her when she walked into the room, Valerie turns to look at him with shock in her eyes.

"Why would you do that? I thought we agreed this is just some sick joke, and you shouldn't give the person who did it the satisfaction of acknowledging it," she says.

"I know that's how you feel about it, but I can't just pretend I didn't find these things. They might be a joke, but they might not be. Sam asked for anything that had to do with these children, anything at all, to be brought to his attention. I think this qualifies as that."

"All you found is some pictures and words that don't mean anything. Everyone around here knows you're a reporter and will likely be covering this case. Someone just wants attention. Making a big deal out of it is going to distract the actual investigation," Valerie says.

"Not necessarily," I tell her. "I admit, this is strange, and you don't see things like this happening all the time, but that doesn't mean it's nothing."

"You did the right thing by getting in touch with me," Sam says. "I don't want to miss a single possible detail or clue that could lead us to these children. I'd appreciate if you could show us the rest of the papers."

Valerie lets out a sigh of exasperation and starts out of the room.

"You're welcome to stay," I call after her.

She turns back around slowly and looks at me with a condescending smile.

"No thank you," she says. "I have more to do with my day than to waste it on a prank. Vincent, is Singer up?"

"Singer?" I ask.

"Our son," Vincent explains. He looks over at his wife. "Not yet. He was up late last night, so I thought I'd let him get some extra sleep."

"You can't let him sleep the day away. That's not good for him," she says.

"It's only seven-thirty," I say before I think through it.

Sam looks at me, then flashes a smile toward Valerie.

"Exactly. And it's summer," he says.

"Be that as it may, I won't allow my son to be lazy. Just because he's not in school during the summer months that doesn't mean he should just turn his brain off. He's attending a day camp through the library this month. By the time he goes back to school in September, he'll be well on his way toward reading through the classics. I find that a bit more beneficial than him lying around the house."

Having made her point, she whips her dark red hair around and stalks out of the room.

"Don't mind her," Vincent says. "She doesn't want to get involved. This is something she's always worried about."

"Children going missing?" I ask.

"Not exactly. I mean, I think every mother worries about that. I'm talking about me getting wrapped up in one of the cases I'm following. She thinks I put too much of myself into it, and it's going to catch up with me," he says.

"I thought she said she thought it's just a joke," Sam says.

"And I think part of her really believes that," Vincent nods. "She doesn't want to take it seriously. It worries her."

"She might have something to worry about. These two pictures together are obviously referencing Alice Brooks. It could be just like she said, a sick joke, someone trying to get attention. Or it could be something a lot more serious. Whoever's responsible for her disappearance could have chosen you to act as a messenger. The question is why," I say. "Show us the other papers."

Vincent moves the drawings and pulls out three more documents. The first is a copy of the camp schedule for the night Alice disappeared. A blue highlighter draws attention to the blank space after 'Lights Out'. The second is a packing list distributed to the parents of the campers. The word 'hammock' has been added into the personal equipment section in the same blocky print as the envelope. The final piece of paper has words typed in huge bold font.

"'She's sleeping beneath the stars,'" Sam reads. "Vincent, we're going to take these with us. Thank you so much for getting in touch. For now, please keep this to yourself."

"I can't print anything about it?" he asks.

"Not yet," Sam tells him. "I need to keep this from the public. Don't tell anyone or print anything until I tell you."

He stacks the papers and slips them into the envelope. We rush out of the house and into his car. Sam is already on his radio by the time my seatbelt clicks into place.

"I need every available officer and volunteer search party members. Organize searches of every field, empty lot, and campground in the area. Make sure there is a uniform at all locations."

He ends the transmission and starts driving toward the station.

"Is her sleeping bag missing?" I ask.

"What?" he asks, looking over at me.

"Her sleeping bag. When you searched through her belongings at camp, did you find her sleeping bag?"

"Yes. It was with her other gear."

I reach into the envelope and pull the papers out again.

"Sam, turn around."

"What?"

"Turn around. We need to go to the camp."

"The camp has already been searched. I think we need to focus on more open spaces," he says.

"No, Sam. We need to go to the camp and search again," I tell him.

"Why?" he asks.

We stop at a light, and I hold the papers out in front of him.

"Because this doesn't say she's sleeping under the stars. Look at it more closely." I run my finger along the heavily bolded word. "The font has been condensed. The space between the letters has been reduced down until it's almost invisible, but it's there."

"What is?" he asks.

"An 'I'. It doesn't say 'stars'. It says 'stairs'. She's sleeping beneath the *stairs*."

CHAPTER SIXTEEN

HIM

W here was she?

Anger burned on the back of his neck and made each heartbeat feel like the pounding of a war drum through his hollow chest. She wasn't where she was supposed to be. Her name was right there, written on the reservation. Nothing fake. Nothing veiled. Nothing undercover. It was her name, the one he had spoken countless times. The one he'd let roll through his mind many more. Emma Griffin.

He knew her travel plans as well as she did, had checked them several times and confirmed the details to make sure he didn't miss her at any stop along the way. He needed to keep his eye on her. He couldn't just let her be out there alone, without him close by. Even if she didn't know he was there, he did. He couldn't help but hope there was a part of her that sensed it, that knew he was nearby and that she was under his watchful eye. She had already been through so much. She felt alone for many years of her life and likely frequently wondered if there was anyone she could completely rely on.

She had to wonder that. Of course she did. It wouldn't make sense if she didn't. There was so much betrayal in her past. All the stories she was told, all the lies people led her to believe until she didn't know what was real and what wasn't. She grew to understand some of it. Some of those stories were thrown away years ago when she opened her eyes and realized what was really happening around her. But in many more ways, she was still in the dark. She didn't know the extent to which her mind was twisted, how much her world was manipulated and changed to suit the needs of others around her without any regard for her future. Or her sanity. She didn't even know who she was.

And now he couldn't find her. Despite all his planning and the careful way he mapped out his journey to ensure he never let Emma get too far away, he had lost track of her. He was at the airport when she was supposed to land. He wanted badly to be standing there waiting for her when she stepped off the plane. He could hold up a sign the way her friend from the Bureau did. She would be so surprised, and with the whole vacation ahead of her, they would have all the time to talk. He could answer her questions. She could answer his.

But he couldn't. Still couldn't. He would have to be satisfied by being in the terminal and watching her walk from the plane, her carry-on over her shoulder. She wasn't one of those women who dressed up to travel like they were still stuck in a generation that was long since irrelevant. Her small collection of high heels and the dresses, skirts, and suits that took up the back half of her closet were relegated to work and very special occasions. Everything else meant a simple wardrobe that left her comfortable, if not glamorous. Yet she still managed to look elegant. People looked at her as she passed not because of the effect of her clothes or bold makeup. They looked at her because it was impossible not to. Emma always had a presence that took up the space around her unapologetically. She didn't wither or blend. Even when perhaps, she should have. He admired her for that. He loved to watch the way people reacted to her without her realizing it was happening.

He'd watch and think to himself: mine.

But when the plane touched down, and the doors opened, she wasn't there. He traveled ahead of her, which meant it was possible she missed her flight or chose another one without him knowing. He went to her hotel and waited for her to check-in, but she never did. Late that night, he approached the desk clerk and told her who he was and asked for her room number. The young man would have given it to him. Of course he would have. He had no reason not to. But Emma had never checked in.

Something was wrong. It had to be. She planned this vacation weeks ago and was looking forward to it. She wouldn't just decide not to go. Something must have happened to her. He shouldn't have gone ahead of her. It was too risky. It kept his eyes off her for too long. The last time he did that, the results were almost catastrophic. He didn't want anything like that to happen again. He took care of it then, but the next time neither of them might be so lucky. He had to find her to make sure she was safe. He was the only one who knew her, the only one who could protect her.

Now he was back in town, but he couldn't find her here, either. As far as he could tell, she wasn't at home. Her car wasn't in the driveway, and nothing seemed to have changed in the house. He couldn't get too close. There were police crawling around the area, and he never knew when they'd be there. If they were a 24-hour surveillance, it would be easier to circumvent them. He could learn their patterns and find ways to get past them far more easily when they were always there than if they only showed up occasionally. Their random appearances shook him and made it harder for him to plan. He needed to find a way to get into the house again. He might be able to find where she went.

This would never have happened if her mother had listened to him.

CHAPTER SEVENTEEN

"Everywhere. I need you to be absolutely sure you have searched every place where there are stairs of any kind. The dining hall, cabins, bleachers, the dock. Even if it doesn't seem immediately like a flight of stairs, check."

The teams nod at me and a few mumble acknowledgments of what I said before they split off in different directions to cover the sprawling space of the camp. All the children were sent off the camp property for the day, so the searches could go unimpeded. Sam didn't want to pull all the search teams out of the other locations, so we only have a handful of people to help us search the grounds. He and I start at the most centralized spot, the camp office. This is where Sandy Brooks, the girl's mother, found out her daughter was missing and where several interviews and investigations have already occurred. It's unfathomable to think Alice could be right here, just tucked out of sight, and has gone unnoticed. But you can never be too sure about anything. You can never just make the assumption that everything is as it seems or as it should be. That's when things are missed.

We start at the front of the office cabin and together search under the steps leading up to the small porch. They are made of simple slats of wood arranged in an open structure that make it easy to see directly under the porch. The clouds have burned away in the morning sunlight somewhat, but it's still hazy, creating shadows and making pockets of darkness that are hard to see through. Sam shines a strong flashlight through the steps and sweeps the beam back and forth through the space. I'm braced for finding something even though I know the chances of Alice being under the office all along are very slim. It takes only a few seconds to eliminate the porch and that set of stairs. There's nothing beneath it but dried leaves.

Continuing around the edge of the building, we come to the back door and the two steps that go up to it. Even more quickly, we eliminate that space as well. Next, we move on to the nearby dining hall. It's a much larger building, and the porch on the front stretches the width of it. Sam and I separate and go to opposite ends of the porch. Pulling out the flashlight he gave me out of the trunk of his car when we got to camp, I shine the bright beam into the corners and then let it spread out wider. It meets Sam's beam in the middle. The pool of illumination reveals nothing.

The clouds keep the glare of the sunlight out of my eyes, but the oppressive humidity is still there, and after two hours of searching, I'm soaked with sweat. I guzzle through a bottle of water and refill it at an outdoor faucet, taking a second to splash a handful on my face to rejuvenate me. So far, we've found nothing. The teams have covered all the cabins where the campers sleep during the sessions, paying particular attention to the one where Alice was last seen. They've scoured the recreation buildings, the counselors' quarters, and the sports fields. Some have roamed deeper into the woods to go to the lake, where they'll check under the dock designed to help young swimmers step down easily into the pool, and the boathouse filled with stacks of platforms and racks holding various watercraft.

Sam walks up beside me and reaches around to fill his own bottle.

"Anything?" I ask.

He shakes his head after gulping his own water down. "No sign of anything."

"Have you heard from the teams outside of the camp?"

"They haven't seen anything, either," he says. "They're going to start searching public buildings next."

I shake my head. "I still think we're supposed to be here. Those papers were chosen purposely. Whoever sent them to Vincent had a specific meaning for each one. Let me look at them again."

Sam takes the envelope out of the backpack slung on his back and hands it to me. Stepping into the shade of a small event pavilion, I empty the papers out into my hand and spread them on a picnic table. I move the two drawings to the side and lay the other three out.

"This highlighter," he says, pointing out the streak of blue across the bottom of the page. "Do you think Alice put it there?"

"No. It's part of the message. It's bringing attention to the time after 'Lights Out'. Remember the girl who told the counselors Alice was missing said she saw Alice go to bed, but then when she woke up a little while later to go to the bathroom, her bed was empty. This was when she was taken."

"But we already knew that. Why would he point out when he took her?" Sam asks.

I shake my head, looking at the other papers. "He didn't. That's not the point. It's not just about this piece of paper. The two drawings went together. Alice and Brooks. The schedule isn't about letting us know what she was doing or when she was taken. It's a part of a message. That's why I asked about the sleeping bag."

"What do you mean?"

"Look here. The packing list has everything the campers are supposed to bring with them, but 'hammock' is added onto it." I look over at Sam, who stares back through his intensely green eyes, confusion written all over him.

Then something hits me. "I know where she is."

Sam chases behind me as I rush back toward the parking area near the office.

"Emma, what's going on?" Sam asks, climbing into the passenger seat beside me.

"Give me your keys," I say.

He reaches into his pocket and pulls out his keys. I snatch them and stick them in the ignition, shooting out of the parking space as soon as the engine turns over.

"Where are we going? What did you figure out?"

"She didn't have her sleeping bag with her, which is what most campers sleep in when they're camping, right?" I ask.

"Yes."

He sounds unsure, but he's listening to me.

"And if she's not in her sleeping bag, it's unlikely she's going to be somewhere on the ground. The 'I' in the word was intentionally hard to see. He wanted people to think it was 'stars' because that's what campers do. They sleep under the stars. All three of these are linked. She was taken after Lights Out to sleep under the stars, but not really. She's not going to be out in a field or at a campground. She's going to be somewhere with something she didn't have when she arrived at camp… a hammock. Do you remember the summer before you left for college, and you took me on a hike?"

"I thought I knew the area and didn't bring a map with me. We got lost and ended up in a cave in the middle of the mountain," he muses. "It rained, and we stayed in the cave until the middle of the night."

"It wasn't just a cave. There was a rock formation over it. When we finally got back, you looked at the map of the area and found the rock formation. It was nowhere near where we meant to go in the first place, but it was really nice, and you wanted to be able to go back sometime. It was flat rocks sticking out of the side of the mountain, leading up to a plateau at the top. Do you remember what it was called?"

I look over at Sam and see his face go gray.

"The Stairway to Heaven."

Sam doesn't try to conceal the pain in his eyes and the weight on his shoulders when he walks up to the podium this time. Murmurs ripple through the group of reporters gathered in front of him as he stares down at his hands gripping the sides of the stand and draws in a long breath. I wish there was something I could do to help him, but I'm relegated behind him. He has to do this on his own.

"A tip received this morning led to the investigation of a previously unsearched area just outside of town. This mountain area was not considered an area of interest due to the information we had at the time. Upon searching the area, we uncovered a set of human remains. Her body was tightly wrapped in a hammock hanging inside a cave. The body is in an advanced stage of decomposition, but preliminary examinations suggest these are the remains of ten-year-old Alice Brooks. Obviously, this is not the conclusion we were hoping for in this case. The team is actively investigating, and our focus is on finding out who did this to Alice while also doing everything we can to bring Caleb and Eva home. Our thoughts and prayers are with the Brooks family. Please respect their privacy during this extremely difficult stage. There will be no questions at this time."

Sam leaves the podium among a flurry of protests, but he doesn't care. He owes nothing to the reporters. They weren't there when we scrambled up the narrow stone pathway in the mountain. They didn't breathe in the tainted air that was the first indication we were getting close to Alice. They aren't the ones who saw the twisted hammock sagging from hooks driven into the rocks.

The image of the dark fluids pooled at the bottom of the swell wrapped in the fabric and the sinking knowledge it was her will never leave him.

It will never leave me, either.

CHAPTER EIGHTEEN

I stand in the shower for as long as the hot water holds out. The steam of the heat and the sound of the water streaming around me creates a buffer that guards me from everything outside. I just want to stay in here, but soon the water cools, and the steam starts to fade out of the room. I climb out and wrap myself in a thick white towel. The management company put them in the closet after the last renters moved out, wanting to create a homey atmosphere for other potential renters. They've never been touched, but now I've claimed them as mine.

I walked into the bathroom as soon as Sam brought me home, which means I have no clothes to change into. The ones piled on the floor won't ever touch my skin again. I fully plan on tossing them into the trash as soon as I can bring myself to touch them again. I don't want the reminder of helping Sam bring the hammock down.

Wrapped in the towel, I walk out of the bathroom and into the bedroom just a few steps away. When I'm dressed in stretch pants and a t-shirt, the smell of peppermint tea lures me downstairs and into the kitchen. Sam's standing beside the stove, staring at a red enamel teapot sitting on the front burner. He doesn't notice me coming into the room.

I watch him for a few seconds. He was one of the things I relied on the most about Sherwood, one of the things I looked forward to most. Older than me by two years, he was always sweet and magnetic. I could rely on him for a deep, meandering conversation about topics most other people my age didn't want anything to do with, but also for an unpredictable laugh. We spent as much time together as we could, but it got harder as the stretches I was away got longer. I never worried what it was going to be like when I finally found my way back to him. Because I was always going to.

No matter how long it was, the moment we saw each other again, it was like there had been no separation at all. We'd pick up our conversation like one of us had just taken a breath and settle right back into the comfortable, easy flow of our friendship. It was much harder than I could have ever expected when he left for college. We'd already been apart. Many times. But it was different when he was the one who left. I didn't know how long it would be to see him again, and by the time I did, everything had changed. I wasn't the same person.

The next time I walked away from him, it would be for seven years.

Sam glances over and realizes I'm there. He turns to me, and our eyes linger on each other.

"You're still here," I say.

"I wanted to make sure you're okay," he tells me.

"I'm not."

He shakes his head. "Neither am I."

Holding mugs of the fragrant, soothing tea, we make our way back into the living room and sit on the couch. There are words waiting to be said between us.

"What did you mean about your vacation being therapist recommended?" Sam finally asks. I let out a breath, my eyes dropping to the floor. "I'm sorry. That's none of my business. You probably don't want to talk about it."

I shake my head, running my fingers back through my hair as I lean forward to set my mug down.

"No, it's fine. Um." I try to decide exactly how to tell him and realize I just have to let the words happen. "Four months ago, I went undercover for an assignment. It was the first time I was in the field for six months."

"What was the assignment?" he asks.

"Hunting a serial killer. He killed more than fourteen people. The investigators are still trying to determine exactly how many victims there actually were." I let out a breath. "Have you heard the name Jake Logan?"

His eyes widen. "Emma…"

I turn my head slightly away from him, not wanting his sympathy.

"It wasn't an easy experience for me. I was taken out of the field because of some things I was going through, and after going through what I did with Jake, I had a hard time bouncing back completely. I've been having nightmares. Flashbacks. My boss decided it would be best for me if I started therapy to help me through the issues of my past and that experience."

"Your father is still missing," he says with calm understanding.

Few people know the full story of when my father disappeared. But it was Sam's arms I fell into when the rest of my world was falling apart.

"Yes. No one has heard from him in ten years," I say.

"I can't believe it's been that long."

I nod. "And a year ago, my boyfriend disappeared. My ex-boyfriend. He broke up with me right before he went missing."

"I'm sorry."

"So, as you can imagine, there has been a lot for the therapist to unpack. She thought a vacation was a good opportunity to relax and relieve some stress."

"I've never seen anything like that. I can't even begin to imagine what that put you through."

"It's my job," I tell him, picking up my tea again and staring down into the mug. "This is what I signed up for. It's what I'm made for. The risks are just part of it."

"No, Emma," Sam says. He reaches over and brushes a strand of hair away from my face, tucking it behind my ear. I turn to look at him. "This may be what you chose, but it doesn't mean you have to just swallow everything down. Being strong doesn't mean not feeling."

He goes quiet, but our eyes stay locked on each other.

"What?" I say softly several seconds later.

"I can still see you," he says.

"What do you mean?" I ask.

He gives me a faint smile. "I can still see you. The girl who wanted to be an artist and created the most incredible things I've ever seen. The one who could talk all night about the tiniest details in movies."

My chest tightens, and my breath catches in my throat as Sam leans toward me. I see the kiss on his lips. I stop myself before I can take it.

"That's not who I am anymore," I whisper.

Sam pulls away and lets his head hang for a second. When he lifts it again, he sets his tea down.

"I think I'm going to go," he says. "I should try to get some sleep."

We stand up, and I follow him to the door.

"We need to go talk to Vincent tomorrow," I say.

He nods in agreement. "I'll pick you up in the morning."

The house feels emptier when I close the door behind him. My nightmares didn't follow me, but that might be because my past has its own ghosts here.

Vincent's face looks drawn when he opens the door. We got a later start this morning than yesterday, but it's still early enough for some of the neighbors on his street to be making their way to work. A few pause at their cars, curiosity drawing their eyes over to us. They don't say anything, but they're hoping to hear something.

There isn't a single person in this town who hasn't heard what happened yesterday. Even if they didn't watch the press conference, the news would have trickled to them from their families, their neighbors. Mothers share the fear with other mothers. Fathers threaten war to hide their own. Grandparents lament a simpler time when something like this wouldn't happen, even though they know this is a threat that transcends generations. They're all waiting for anything to grasp onto. Sherwood is holding its breath.

"I thought you might come today," Vincent says through a long exhale. He steps back away from the door. "Come in."

Valerie comes down the stairs angrily, lashing the sash of her bathrobe around her waist as she glares at us.

"What are you doing here?" she demands. "Don't you think you've put my husband through enough?"

"We didn't put your husband through anything," Sam says.

"You can't possibly still think that envelope was a joke," I say. "It led to the body of a murdered ten-year-old girl."

She crosses her arms over her chest defensively.

"What are you suggesting?"

"I'm not suggesting anything. I'm making a statement, and that statement is someone who knows a lot about a murdered child sent clues to Vincent, and we want to know why."

"Do you have a warrant?" she asks.

"Valerie, please," Vincent says.

"No. They're invading our privacy. They're harassing you. All our neighbors have seen them in front of our house two days in a row now. You don't think they're going to start making that connection?"

"This isn't about Vincent right now," Sam cuts in. "This is about a little girl named Alice Brooks, who lost her life in a brutal, horrible way and two other children who are still missing. This guy chose Vincent for some reason, which means he might be the strongest clue we have."

Valerie glares at Sam like she wants to say something, then turns away in a huff and stalks into the living room to the side. I watch her search a large bookcase and finally select one of the hundreds of volumes filling the shelves. She picks up a small notebook and pen from a small table set beside the case and stalks back up the steps.

"Come sit down," Vincent says in the wake of a door slamming closed over our heads.

We sit in the living room she just left, and I look to Sam to start the conversation.

"Is there anything else you know that you haven't told us, Vincent?" he asks.

Vincent shakes his head and holds his hands out as if to show they're empty.

"Nothing. I called you as soon as I found that envelope yesterday. What you saw is all I know."

"You have no idea who left the envelope?" I ask.

"No. It was just there when I opened the door."

"Do you have any way of checking? Surveillance cameras? A video doorbell? A neighbor who might have been out that early and seen something?"

"No. As you might have caught on to by now, Valerie is a very private person. She hates the idea of any kind of camera, even if it's supposed to be recording other people. She watched an expose on those cameras and how they get hacked. All she can think about is someone watching her while she's going around the house or out in the yard."

We talk for a few more minutes but don't get any new information before we stand up to leave. Sam shakes Vincent's hand and gets reassurance he will call if he hears anything else. He opens the door to let us out and then quickly closes it.

"What's going on?" Sam asks.

"Jennings is out there," Vincent mutters. He walks over to the window that looks out over the yard and pulls it aside just enough to peer out. "Son of a bitch."

"What is he doing here?" Valerie asks in a hiss as she comes back down the stairs.

She's dressed now, but her expression hasn't changed.

"I don't know," Vincent says.

"Do you see what you're causing?" she asks Sam. "I don't want my family out in the scrutiny of the public eye."

"I've already told him to back off," he tells her.

She narrows her eyes. "Then do better."

CHAPTER NINETEEN

"Valerie, please," Vincent begs.

"No, Vincent. I'm not going to let this town turn on us because we end up in the news. You handed over that information. Your involvement is over now. But if the Sheriff can't stop William Jennings from interfering with our lives..." her voice trails off, but the look in her eyes is enough to say the rest for her.

I notice she's clutching the book she took from the bookshelf in her hand, and now she brings it to her chest, holding it tightly to her heart like it somehow strengthens her. Sam gives a single nod and walks through the front door and out onto the porch. I follow him, making sure the door closes behind me before Jennings can get any shots of the inside of the house. I can't do anything about Vincent standing at the window and peering out through the curtains, but I block as much of the door with my body as I can and hope both husband and wife stay inside.

"I thought I told you to stay out of this," Sam frowns as he strides purposefully toward Jennings.

The bright-eyed reporter leans back against his black car and gives a cocky smile.

"And I thought I told you I have freedom of the press, Sheriff," Jennings says. "This is an important story, don't you agree?"

"Of course it's an important story. That's why you need to stay out of it. You could compromise our investigation, not to mention invading the privacy of his family on their own property."

"I'm not on their property. I've stayed on the street. Anything I'm able to see is fair game to the public. I'm sure you know that," Jennings tells him.

"You need to back off," I say. "You might think being part of the press gives you some sort of invincible shield, but it doesn't. Interfering with an investigation is just as illegal for you as it is for anyone else."

He looks me up and down in the same type of slimy way he did when I first met him.

"FBI," he says like it's my name. "I've been looking into you. Your career has been pretty impressive."

"I know," I say flatly, refusing to give him any hint that he's flattered me or that I care at all about his opinion.

"You need to pack up your camera and leave," Sam says. "You have access to the press conferences just like everyone else, but you're not going to harass people to concoct some sort of story."

"I don't need to concoct a story," Jennings says. "A local reporter getting the clues that proved to be the turning point in a child murder case is all the story I need. That is until I get to reveal the murderer."

"How did you know that?" Sam asks. "We didn't release any details about the tip we received to the public."

Jennings smiles a little wider and licks his lips as he pushes away from the car.

"I have my ways, Sheriff. Look around you. There are people everywhere. They're watching. It's just a matter of knowing how to ask."

"You are not to discuss Vincent, his family, or any information about the tip we received in any way. Do you understand me? If I catch a single hint that you've put his name out there or gone to press with something that could compromise the integrity of our investigation or cause them any problems, I will not hesitate to arrest you and petition the court to silence you."

Sam glares him down, and finally, Jennings shakes his head and stuffs his equipment onto the passenger seat of his car before getting behind the wheel. His tires squeal as he pulls out of his parking spot and disappears further into the neighborhood.

Sam and I get into his car and start in the opposite direction. We are planning on spending the day interviewing the families of the missing children again. They've all talked about the children and the circumstances surrounding their disappearances exhaustively, but there's always the chance they forgot something or didn't mention a detail because it didn't seem important at the time, but now know to say it. I also didn't get a chance to be a part of the initial interviews, and I would like to hear what they have to say from their own mouths. A person's voice and the way they hold themselves can speak even more than the words they're actually saying.

My mother was that way. She could seem totally invested in a conversation and be as pleasant as she could be in the words she was saying, but the way she held her body expressed her true emotions. From the time I was very young, I learned to identify who I could trust by the way my mother held herself when she spoke to them.

A few minutes into the ride, I look over at Sam.

"What's with Jennings? Because from everything I'm seeing, it's more than just someone who is a little bit overzealous about getting a story. Especially between him and the Lams."

"That's probably true. Like I said, he's originally from around here. Not that he acts like he remembers."

"So, this is a he got too big for his britches situation," I say.

Sam chuckles. "I think you're the only person I know who would actually put it that way, but it's accurate. He seems to enjoy throwing his success in Vincent's face. There's always been competition between them, and a lot of people think Vincent never really got over Jennings getting to cover bigger stories, getting notoriety, and making so much more money. Being able to tell such a dramatic story that will not only draw in huge audiences because it's about children but also smears Vincent a little is like a dream to Jennings. He'll do anything he has to do to make sure he's the one to tell the story, but also the one who gets to decide how it's told."

"Can I ask you something else? Something maybe a little personal?" I ask.

"Sure," he says.

"What about Valerie?"

"What about her?" Sam asks.

"Have you ever had anything to do with her? I mean on a personal level?"

He snaps an incredulous look in my direction, then turns back to the street and lets out a short, disbelieving laugh.

"Valerie and me? Absolutely not. Why would you think that?"

"She's just so bristled, so on edge. It seems particularly directed to you," I point out.

"That's just Valerie. She's been that way for as long as I've known her, which is essentially always. She's always been really in her head if you know what I mean. Very serious."

"That explains the book she picked out of the bookcase. I had to read that thing in college. It was like wading through quicksand while trying to hack my way through a jungle with a machete outfitted with a rubber safety edge," I tell him. "I love to read, but that writing is dense. And dry. it's tough to get through."

"So kind of like brownies," Sam shrugs. "Somebody out there loves them, but it's pretty tough to get through when they are dense and dry."

"That sounds like the teenage boy I used to know. Leave it to you to be able to distill any complicated issue down into the universal language of baked goods," I say.

We share a slight smile. It's just enough to soften the discomfort of what we're going through, but not enough for the tension to disappear.

"Jennings, on the other hand…" his voice trails off, but I'm not about to let that go.

"What do you mean? Jennings and Valerie?"

"I don't know for absolute certain. I didn't walk in on them or anything, but there have been a few rumors that have gone around that the two of them were fraternizing with the enemy, so to speak," he says. "But that was years ago."

Sam turns back to the road in front of us, and my eyes lift to the rearview mirror to check behind us for Jennings. He seemed to hear the threat Sam issued, but I don't know how much impact it actually made. I'm waiting for his car to appear behind us and for him to try to insert himself in our interviews. He doesn't sit well with me. He's too malleable, a chameleon who changes his attitude and the energy of his presence as easily as he changes who he's looking at. I've dealt with his kind before, and they can make difficult investigations even harder.

Now that the rumor of him being involved with Valerie is in my mind, him prowling around is an even more uncomfortable situation. There's definitely such a thing as an unfounded rumor, and I've found myself the fodder for them before. But Valerie makes me doubt there isn't at least some validity to the whispers. Someone who lashes out so aggressively toward people invading her family's privacy and questioning her husband's integrity wouldn't just sit by and let people say things like that about her. But she would also be unlikely to fight too hard, or people might start searching out ways to prove themselves right. In this situation, silence might just be an admission of guilt.

The first house we pull up to is too quiet. I expect there to be cars parked haphazardly around it and people filtering in and out, trying to find their footing, not knowing what to do. Instead, there's no one. A single car sits close to the front of the driveway next to a pink and white bike that makes my heart fall into my stomach.

I steel myself as I unhook my seatbelt and climb out of the car into the heat. The clouds burned away this morning without bothering to rain. The bright sunlight is intrusive, like glitter on the sidewalk, inappropriate as we walk up to the door and knock.

CHAPTER TWENTY

The door opens quickly, almost as though Sandy Brooks was standing there waiting for the knock. She looks out at us with a look of stone in her eyes and a strong, cold face streaked with unapologetic tears.

"Sheriff," she says. "Please, come in."

"Thank you, Sandy."

I follow Sam into the house and notice a man standing in the arched doorway leading from the front room to the dining room beyond. He nods as we enter and walks around us to get to Ms. Brooks. She reaches for his hand, and he grasps hers in both of his, leaning close to speak to her in a hushed town.

"Who is that?" I ask as Sam leads me to the far side of the room, so we don't interfere with the interaction.

"Patrick Robins, the pastor at the church," he whispers back.

The pastor leaves, and Ms. Brooks wipes a tear from under her eye as she crosses the room to us.

"Go ahead and sit down," she says, gesturing toward a formal-looking floral couch. "Let me get you some water. It's far too hot out there."

"You don't need to do that," Sam says.

"Yes," she says with a nod, "I do."

"Can I help you?" I ask.

She shakes her head. "I might not be able to do much right now, but I can still pour water."

She walks out of the room, and I look down at the oversized rose print on the cream background of the couch. I can't help but wonder if there's another room deeper in the house where the couch is soft and worn and smells like warmth and food, mother and daughter rather than starkly clean. The family couch versus the company couch, a perfect example of what you show to the world and what you keep only to yourself.

The sound of glass shattering breaks me out of my musing, and I'm instantly on my feet. My heart thudding in my chest, and memories of bullets searing a path through the air toward my head brings my hand to my hip.

But my gun isn't there. I'm not on assignment. I have no weapon.

When I get to the kitchen, I realize I don't need it. The window isn't broken, and Sandy Brooks isn't cowering on the floor, trying to protect herself from an attack. She's standing at the counter, looking down at pieces of glass scattered across the linoleum.

"Are you alright?" I ask, cautiously stepping into the room.

Her head pops up, and she looks at me almost startled, then nods.

"Yes. I'm sorry. I just… I dropped the glass."

I reach over the area of the floor covered in the remnants of the glass and take her shoulders. Guiding her around the shards, I hand her off to Sam so he can bring her back into the living room while I clean up the mess. I grab a handful of paper towels and wet them in the sink, so they'll pick up the tiny pieces of glass. From the living room, I hear Sam talking to her in softened tones. The conversations we have to have today are delicate, but they have to be done. I finish cleaning up the aftermath of her unpredictable emotions and make my way back to them with water in plastic tumblers I found in an upper cabinet.

"I'm willing to answer anything you need me to," she's saying as I enter. "I have nothing to hide."

"Of course you don't," Sam says.

I bristle at the response. He's trying to be reassuring, but I've learned far too well that in many cases comfort comes before the fall. Everyone has something to hide.

"Can you tell me everything that happened the day and night leading up to you finding out Alice was missing?" I ask.

She looks at me, and I wonder if she's even really seeing me or if my voice is coming to her through blackness and painful images of her child.

"I've already given that statement," she says.

"But not to me," I tell her.

"Who are you?" she asks.

"Emma Griffin. I'm with the FBI. I'm consulting on this case with Sheriff Johnson," I tell her.

"The investigation has changed now, Sandy," Sam says. "I've built up a task force, and we're shifting our focus. But that means starting from the beginning in a lot of ways."

She nods faintly. As sheriff, Sam was elected to be the top of law enforcement in Sherwood. It's his job to determine how crimes are investigated and manage peace within the population. I know he has a strong team behind him, but I also know him. He was telling the truth when he said asking for help was hard for him. He will run himself into the ground taking on everything himself just so he knows it's being done right. I won't take for granted that he reached out to me.

I listen as she recounts the day she learned Alice was missing. She does what many people do in interviews like this, swinging from giving us minute details like everything she bought at the grocery store to generalizing large swaths of time. I try to fill in the gaps as much as I can, but much of that day is lost in the blur of her new reality.

"What about Alice's father?" I ask.

"That's not a word I'd use to describe him," she mutters. "He hasn't had anything to do with Alice since the day he walked out."

"Was that his choice?" I ask.

Her eyes narrow. "What do you mean by that?"

"I don't mean any offense. It's just that most people believe they would be able to manage co-parenting and being cordial to each other for the sake of children if their relationship ended. When it actually happens, though, it turns out to be much harder than they expected."

"I didn't use my daughter as a weapon if that's what you're implying."

"I'm not implying anything. It was a question," I say.

"We're just trying to get the full view of everyone in Alice's life," Sam explains. "Finding the person responsible for this is going to be like putting together a puzzle, and we need all the pieces."

Her shoulders lower as she lets out a breath.

"Brad and I didn't part on good terms. It wasn't a smooth break, and by the time it was finally over, I felt like I'd been put through a meat grinder. We never got to the point of making formal arrangements for custody or visitation. As soon as the divorce was finalized, he walked out of the courthouse and has barely been heard from since."

"Why did you keep his name?" I ask.

A slight bitter smile curves up the corner of her mouth.

"I grew up with my mother having a different last name than me. She was a fiercely independent woman who didn't marry until she was well into her thirties, and by then, she made up her mind she wasn't going to take any man's last name. I never understood why, but it gave her some sort of sense of pride to hang onto her name. I remember her loving to correct people when they called her Mrs. Bevins. Her spine would straighten up, and she would get this very pitying look on her face, then tell them she was *Ms. Foster*. I found it ridiculous, and I know it hurt my father's feelings. Not necessarily that she chose to keep her name, though he didn't like that, but that she would be so adamant and forceful about correcting people. Like it was somehow offensive to her to be linked to him that way. The whole thing embarrassed me so much. Her correcting people. People wondering why we didn't have the same name. The judgement. The questioning stares. I had kids at school ask me if my father was really my father, or if my mother was my stepmother, then not be able to wrap their heads around it when I told them no."

She takes a sip of her water and clears her throat.

"So, when it was time for me to get married, I knew that's not what I was going to do. None of that nonsense for me. I was going to take his name, and we would be a family. A real cohesive unit. There wasn't a single second when I wondered what would happen if we got divorced. That didn't even cross my mind. Then when it happened, I had to make a decision. Either I would fully sever the connection I had with Brad by taking my maiden name back, or I would save my daughter the discomfort and possible humiliation of having a mother with a different last name. It wasn't a hard choice. I'm not a Mrs. anymore, but I still have his name. I can't excise him fully from my life and pretend it never happened. The name is mine now. It's not property to be divided up and given back to him. He didn't gift it to me, and I'm not going to cut it away like I'm slinking back to life before him. I changed when I married him, and I can't go back. Just forward."

The morning has slipped to afternoon by the time we leave Ms. Brooks' house and continue on to our next interview. I recorded much of what she had to say on my phone, and I upload it to a secure cloud folder so we can review it later.

Our next stop is a street with rows of duplexes and a park on the corner. Children scramble around the park equipment, oblivious in their play. But adults, parents, and grandparents who before might have let them out by themselves now hover around the edge of the playground, like they've created a defense perimeter. Their eyes are on their children, and their minds are on high alert. A block down, there's a woman sitting on the porch of a duplex, her gaze locked on the park, not with watchful care, but with hopeful anticipation.

CHAPTER TWENTY-ONE

V oice Memo:
>   *Kendra Donahue – Caleb's mother*
>   *Emma:* Tell me about Caleb, Mrs. Donahue.

Kendra: Kendra. I'm nobody's Mrs.

Emma: Kendra.

Kendra: Caleb is a good boy. Always has been. He's never gotten caught up in any of the stuff going around kids these days. He just wants to have fun. I might wish he would study a little harder sometimes, but his grades have never gotten too bad, so I don't push him about it. He's only going to be young once, you know? Just one time to be a boy before he has to figure out how to be a man. I don't want him learning those lessons too soon. So, I let him be. All he wants is to play and spend time with his family.

Emma: Is that what he was doing the day he was last seen?

Kendra: Yes. He'd made a new friend at school just a couple of months before the year ended. Caleb loves people. He's always smiling at everyone he passes by on the street and won't ever let anyone sit out. He just wants everyone to have fun and be happy. He knew of this boy for a while, and they were friendly enough, the way most kids are friendly to each other when they're in the same room. But they were assigned a project in class and had to work together for it. That got them closer, and soon, he was always talking about him. He wanted to have a sleepover at his house. I'm not one to let my children do sleep-overs much unless it's family, but since it was summertime, I thought it would be fine. He was going to be away a lot before the new school year started, so I thought he'd like to spend time with his friend before then.

Emma: Who is the friend?

Kendra: Ellis Robins.

Emma: Robins? The pastor's son?

Kendra: Yes. I figured that meant he was in good hands. Pastor wouldn't let them get into any trouble.

Emma: You said he'd be spending a lot of the summer away?

Kendra: We've got a big family. Half the duplexes on this road are family. I have to keep working in the summer, and I don't want my kid alone all day. They go on trips and spend time with their aunts, uncles, and cousins. They'll see their father. It's good for them.

Emma: Is that what you thought happened? He left the sleepover at the Robins' house, and when he didn't come home that night, you figured he was with family?

Kendra: I'm a good mother, Ms. Griffin.

Emma: Emma. I'm not questioning that.

Kendra: Do you have children, Emma?

Emma: No.

Kendra: Then you can't understand what it's like to have your only purpose be getting them through this world. Before you have them, it's all about you, and things don't seem so big or like they matter so much. But then everything changes, and you are carrying these children on your back, never wanting their feet to touch the ground, facing down fire, and seeing evil where you never saw it before. You want to do anything to protect them. You'd draw them in and keep them right beside you every minute if you could, just so nothing happens to them. But you can't. They have to live. So, you let them. You do what you can to trust other people. You're forced to let them go. I have always wanted my son to know his father and be close with him. I want him to have a family that is always there for him and that is so strong and so full of love he doesn't have to try to find validation anywhere else. So, when his father wants to spend time with him, that's where he is. When his uncles and aunts and cousins go on trips and say there's room for him, he's there. I don't make him call home because I want him to live in his moment, and I trust the people he's with. He's as much at home when he's with my sister or his father or my brother as he is when he's right here with me. I thought I was doing right by my son, Emma. And it will always be on my head that I put him down.

V oice Memo:
     Janet and Paul Francis – Eva's grandparents
Janet: Have you heard anything?
Sam: No. Nothing. I'm sorry.
Paul: It's better that way.
Janet: How could you say that?
Paul: If he hasn't heard anything, it means they haven't found her. Not like Alice.
Emma: Is it alright if I ask you a few questions about Eva?
Janet: Of course. I just can't believe you're here. So many years no one heard one word from you, then I look out the window and you're right there. Back across the street like you never left.
Emma: I'm glad to be able to help.
Paul: What do you need to know about Eva?
Emma: You told the officers when she first went missing that she never spent time at home alone. Is that right?
Janet: Yes. Never. We always made sure one of us was home when she got out of school and staggered going into work so that we could see her off to the bus. During the summer, we alternated our days off as much as we could and involved her in as many programs as we could so she would never be at home by herself. That morning was

the first time she was home without one of us. It was only supposed to be for fifteen minutes. Just fifteen minutes.

Paul: She knew not to answer the door for anyone and not to let anyone inside. She wasn't allowed to wait outside for the van. She was to stay inside with the door locked until she saw them drive up, then she could go.

Emma: And she was supposed to be going to a water park that day?

Janet: Yes. With her youth group from church. She was so excited. She'd been talking about it for days. We even went and bought her a brand new bathing suit with matching flip-flops, and sunglasses, and got her a new towel. She had to have packed and unpacked and repacked her bag three times the night before.

Emma: Can I see the bag?

Paul: It's gone. It wasn't here when we got home after getting the call from the pastor that she wasn't there when he came to get her. Wherever she is, she has it with her.

Janet: Do you really think you can find her?

Emma: Sam has a good team behind him, and we're going to do everything we can.

Janet: I know you will. It's so good to see the two of you leaning on each other again. I always thought you two were going to be together. No matter what else was going on, you two were going to make it.

CHAPTER TWENTY-TWO

I turn off the recording, and we sit for a few seconds in silence, letting the worried voices of the families settle into us. Sam sits beside me, his pen poised over a blank page in a notebook. He's been sitting that way since I started replaying the interviews. He hasn't written down a single word.

"How do you deal with stuff like this every day?" he asks.

"What do you mean? This isn't your first murder investigation," I say.

"You're right. It's not. But it is the first time I have seen anything like this and been the one in charge of making it stop. The occasional murder or domestic violence killing is one thing. This is completely different. And I know you've seen it before. How do you deal with it?"

"Because I have to. Because someone has to. Pretending it doesn't exist and not confronting it isn't going to stop sick people from doing these things. It's just going to make it easier for them. I decided a long time ago I was going to be one of the people to stand in their way. I might not always be able to stop lives from being taken, but I can make sure people answer for what they've done," I tell him.

"Is that why you left?" he asks.

"I left to go into training and become an agent."

"That's why you left Sherwood. I meant, is that why you left me?"

"Sam, I can't have this conversation right now."

"Why not?" he asks. "We never had it before. You never gave me a chance. Why not have it now that we're back in the same room together for the first time in seven years?"

"You knew from the time we met up again in college that I was planning on joining the Bureau. It wasn't a surprise."

"It was a surprise, Emma. That wasn't anything like the girl I knew," he says.

"The girl you knew hadn't been through enough yet. She hadn't waited for years for someone to figure out who killed her mother and why. She was murdered right there in our house, and no one was ever able to give me an explanation. Not what really happened to her, or who did it, or why. No one was ever made responsible for that or held accountable for the damage they did to me and to my father. I couldn't just keep letting that happen. If no one else was going to stand up for my mother, I was going to. When my father disappeared, it just solidified what I was supposed to do with my life. It might not be what everyone expected, but that doesn't matter."

"That still doesn't explain why you pushed me away. Why you never came home," he says.

"I did what I had to do. There was no way I was going to be able to move forward in the life I had ahead of me if I kept myself in the past. I had to separate myself from the life I used to lead. This place, this house, even you. If I didn't, I would never be able to be the agent I wanted to be."

"Why not?" he asks.

I let out a sigh. "What did you imagine for us, Sam? What did you see in our future after we graduated from college? Did you see a woman with a gun on her hip hunting serial killers and breaking up drug rings? Or did you see one with a baby on her hip making dinner, always there when you got home?"

He stares at me without saying anything. I give a slight nod. "Exactly."

"I never would have stopped you from doing something that you believed in because of some image I had."

"I know you wouldn't have. That's the thing. You wouldn't have had to. I watched my parents suffer for each other. I watched my mother stay strong even while she missed my father, and cry for him when she was worried about him. I watched my father grieve himself into almost nothing when my mother was murdered. That's not something I ever could have put you through. If I let myself stay with you and keep going, I wouldn't have been able to let you worry about me and think about the danger I was in every day. It would have stopped me from being able to give myself completely to what I needed to do. This place, this world, couldn't be mine if I wanted to be in the Bureau and fight for what I believe in."

His phone rings before Sam can say anything else, and I take a second to catch my breath.

"What?" he snaps into the phone, but a second later, his face drops and he looks over at me.

"What is it?" I ask.

"I'll be right there," he says and ends the call, shoving the phone into his pocket as he stands up from my couch.

"What's going on?"

"We need to get to the station. Another child has gone missing."

The ride to the station is tense with the weight of our conversation and the reality of another child gone sitting heavily on us. He's barely put the car in park when Sam takes off his seatbelt and rushes toward the building. I follow him right past the waiting area and into the back to an interview room where the officer at the front desk tells us 'she' is. I don't know who he was talking about, but as soon as we walk into the room, I see her.

A gorgeous dark-haired woman sits in a hard-plastic chair at the white table, her arms wrapped around herself as she rocks back and forth. Her lips move rapidly, and from the few whispered words I can catch and translate, it sounds like she is praying in Spanish.

"Bianca," Sam says.

She looks up, and her almond eyes widen. In an instant, she's out of the chair and across the room. I'm stunned when she throws herself into Sam's arms and clings to him, one hand gripping the back of his uniform, and her face tucked into his shoulder as she sobs.

"She's gone," she finally gasps. "Gloria's gone."

He holds her for a few seconds, running his hand down the thick hair that hangs to her waist. This isn't the reaction of just a concerned sheriff. My stomach twists. I chastise myself for the reaction and force myself to look away from a moment I feel I shouldn't be a part of. Finally, Sam takes the woman by her upper arms and guides her away from him, easing her back the few steps and into the chair. He gestures to me.

"Bianca, this is Emma Griffin. She's helping me with the investigation."

"I know," Bianca says, sniffling. "I saw you at the press conference. You're an officer, too."

Actually, I'm an FBI agent, I want to correct her, but now's not the time.

"Emma, this is Bianca Hernandez."

"It's nice to meet you."

The sentiment falls hollow and insincere. It's one of those phrases that fall from people's lips without them even having to think about saying them. That come even when they probably shouldn't. I wonder how often people say that and actually mean it.

"Tell me what happened," Sam says, sitting down in the chair beside her and leaning forward on his thighs.

"Gloria was at the community center today. They're doing an art program for a couple of weeks of the summer. Parents drop their kids off before they go to work, and they spend the day trying out different kinds of art and music. She eats lunch there, plays outside, has reading time, then I pick her up when I get off. It was supposed to give her something to do and keep her safe. And you know how much she loves art. She's always sketching or making her own comic books. But today, when I went to pick her up, the director said she was already picked up. Showed me the sign-out sheet and everything."

"Whose name was on the sign-out sheet?" Sam asks.

"Mine," Bianca says almost desperately, holding curled fingers to her chest as she sags over toward her lap. "It was my name, and it even looked like my handwriting, but I didn't sign it. I was at work until fifteen minutes before I got to the center. It was my early day, and I was excited to spend the afternoon with her. All I did was stop for gas between leaving the hospital and getting there."

"The hospital?" I ask.

"I work at the desk in the emergency room," she says.

"Did anyone see who signed the paper? The director or any of the adults supervising the children?" Sam asks.

"No. They say that's the point of the sign-out sheet. They are so busy running around with the kids they don't have time to sit by the door. So, they have the sign-out sheet posted there, and if no one is available when the parent comes, they just sign the sheet themselves," she explains.

"That seems like a tremendous oversight," I point out.

"You have to fill out your child's name, your name, the time you came to get them, and sign it. It seemed like enough of a safeguard," Bianca says.

Sam takes out his notebook.

"I need you to tell me everything you can think of about today. What Gloria was wearing, what she brought to the community center with her, if you got any phone calls, what was going on at the center when you got there, if there were any other names on the sign-out sheet. Everything."

My phone rings, and I look down at the screen. It's an unfamiliar number, but I recognize the area code. It's the same as the number that called me from Feathered Nest.

I nod to Sam to indicate that I need a minute and step out into the hallway.

"Hello?" I say almost breathlessly, bringing the phone up to my ear.

I'm waiting for the emptiness and breathing again. But this time, there's a voice.

"Emma?"

"Yes?"

"This is Clancy. Remember me?"

Air streams from my lungs at the sound of the older man's voice, but I don't know if it's relief or disappointment as I step out of the room.

"Of course I remember you, Clancy. How are you?"

"I hope you don't mind me calling you. It took some poking around to get your right number. That one you had while you were here isn't working anymore."

That's because it was a burner phone attached only to my undercover persona. Clancy, the repairman who came to fix the furnace in the cabin where I stayed during my assignment, would have had to jump through a few hoops and find the right people to get my actual contact information.

"I don't mind, Clancy, but I'm kind of busy right now. Is there something you needed?" I ask.

"I just wanted to let you know I was doing some spring cleaning around Miss Wendy's cabin. Got a little bit of a late start this year," he chuckles. "Anyway, I was raking up under the porch. It seriously needed doing. Haven't touched it since right after the last people rented it. I found something I reckon is yours. Probably dropped it, and it slipped down through the slats of the porch."

"Oh. Thank you. I'll give you my address. You can mail it to me."

"I guess you won't be coming back through Feathered Nest any time soon?"

"No. I'm not planning on it." I give him my address. "Thank you, again. I appreciate it."

I put my phone back in my pocket and go back into the room. Bianca is still talking and doesn't stop until the door to the room bursts open right behind me. I whip around to see Brandy, a young officer who was at the camp searching with us, standing in the doorway with widened eyes.

"Sheriff, we just got a call from Vincent Lam. He needs to speak with you. It's urgent."

CHAPTER TWENTY-THREE

We leave Bianca with Brandy to continue the preliminary stages of the investigation and head back to the car. We don't acknowledge where we're going or what that might mean.

"Who was on the phone?" he asks as we pull out of the parking lot.

"The repairman who takes care of the cabin where I stayed in Feathered Nest," I tell him.

"From Feathered Nest?" Sam asks, sounding both surprised and wary. "Why was he calling you?"

"He was doing some cleaning and maintenance around the cabin and found something under the porch. I must have dropped it while I was there," I say.

"And?"

His tone makes me look at him incredulously.

"And? And he's going to mail it to me. Why do you ask it like that?"

"I can't imagine that's a place you want to think much about anymore. Like you said, it was really hard on you. I just don't like the idea of you still being connected to it."

"You don't like the idea? Why? Because of what my therapist said? Because of the trauma? Or because of Jake?"

I know Sam well enough to know as soon as he found out about my involvement in the case, he would research to find out everything he could about it. Which means he was bound to stumble on the articles that lean heavily into the suggestion about my relationship with Jake. They didn't name me or come right out and say there was something going on between us, but there was enough subtext and clever word choices to make sure readers caught on to exactly what they meant.

His hands tighten on the steering wheel, but he keeps staring straight ahead.

"I just don't think it's a good idea to keep yourself attached to something like that. It's not good to be so personal with your cases."

My jaw tightens, and my throat aches, but I try to refuse to acknowledge either of them. I'd rather focus on him lecturing me and trying to sound like he understands what any of this is like for me. The types of cases we've dealt with and how we've had to deal with them have been completely different. I'd rather sit in my indignance about him drawing lines between them than let myself venture even for a second into why that woman in the interview room bothered me.

"Right. It's never good to get personally invested in your cases," I say.

"Is the sarcasm directed toward Bianca?" he asks.

"I couldn't help but notice she seemed a little friendlier toward you than the other parents. And she assumed you were familiar with her and her daughter's lives. You know the little girl loves art," I say. "How long have you been dating?"

"We're not," he says firmly.

"Does she know that?" I ask with sharpness on my tongue I'm not proud of.

"We did date. But it was a long time ago."

"Is Gloria yours?" I ask.

"No. It wasn't that long ago. Gloria was already five when we started dating. We were together for about a year."

"What happened?"

"Nothing really. It just wasn't working out. There wasn't anything bad between us or anything. We just realized we were on different paths. We separated on good terms," he shrugs.

"It definitely looked like it."

"We were friends before we dated, and nothing happened to make it so we shouldn't be friends now. It's not like we get together and have coffee every week, but we also don't hate each other just because we didn't make it as a couple. Why does it matter to you, anyway?"

The question makes me shift uncomfortably in my seat, and I'm relieved to pull up in front of Vincent's house.

"It doesn't. I just like to be informed of all the details of any case I'm working on, and that includes the personal relationships between people involved. If you were romantically linked to her, it could cloud your judgement and distract you from being able to fully concentrate on searching for these children," I say.

I start to get out of the car, but Sam touches my wrist to stop me.

"Emma," he says.

I look at him for only a beat, then pull my hand away.

"He's at the door waiting for us," I tell him.

"It's happened again," Vincent says as we walk up the sidewalk toward him.

"What's happened?" Sam asks.

He points down at the porch, and as we get closer, I see a manila envelope like the one the papers were in sitting leaned partially against the threshold.

"I worked from home this morning but was going to go into the office for a while this afternoon to go over some story details with the editor. Valerie is gone for the day, and Singer is rock climbing with a friend. The house got really quiet. But as I was leaving, I saw this out here."

"Have you touched it?" Sam asks.

Vincent shakes his head adamantly. "I haven't disturbed it at all. The second I saw it, I went back inside and called the station. I've been watching through the window since to make sure no one got near the porch or moved it."

"So, you don't know what's inside?" I ask.

"No."

Sam goes to the car and comes back wearing gloves. He picks up the envelope and slips it inside a bag.

"Thank you, Vincent. Stay available. We might need to talk to you again," he says.

He nods, and we rush for the car. I hold the envelope in my lap as we drive back to the station. My fingers tingle wanting to open it and find out what's inside. But I don't want to compromise the evidence. The first envelope was opened, and everything emptied out of it before anyone figured out what it was and the importance it held. We can't do the same for this one. We need to be precise and careful processing the envelope and whatever is inside at each stage so it can hopefully be used later to lead us to the person responsible and nail them to the wall.

"What do you think is in here?" I ask.

Sam shakes his head. "I don't know, but we're about to find out. Does it feel like more papers?"

I gently squeeze the envelope, not wanting to damage anything that might be inside.

"There's something solid in there. Something more than just a stack of papers."

My curiosity makes the time it takes to get to the station and photograph the envelope stretch on. Finally, it's time to open it. Sam carefully slits the piece of tape sealing it and pinches together the metal clasp.

"The person who sent this likely used water, but I want the flap tested, anyway. People have done stupider things, and it would be worse for us to be the ones to miss that," he says.

He gets the flap up and carefully tips the envelope over, positioning his hand at the opening to guide the contents onto the table. A small packet falls from the bottom of the envelope into his palm, and he sets it down, then peers into the envelope.

"Anything else?" I ask.

"No. That's it," he tells me.

The officer in the room with us photographs the packet from a few angles before Sam unfolds the paper and unfurls several layers until he's holding a small black object in his hand. I reach over for the paper and look down at it.

"It looks like the crossword puzzle from a newspaper," I observe. "But there's nothing else, no articles or anything."

"They must have wanted something in the envelope to protect this," he muses, holding the object out to me.

"Is that a flash drive?" I ask.

He nods. "There's no label or anything. Should we see what's on it?"

"Do you have any computers that aren't connected to the infrastructure of the department? Anything you don't mind potentially not getting through this experience?"

"What do you mean?"

"A random flash drive sent in the wake of crimes like this could be more evidence. Or it could be a catastrophic virus that would destroy any computer it's put into. It could also be a hacking program that would allow someone access to whatever computer it's opened on. We need to see what's on it, but we need to do it securely," I tell him.

It takes even longer for us to find a computer that's been wiped and separated from the rest of the computer system in the department. Sam inserts the end of the flash drive into the USB and looks at me with slightly raised eyebrows.

"Here we go," he mutters.

He clicks on the icon that appears on the screen, and for a few seconds, nothing seems to happen. Then the screen lightens, and a faint strain of music starts playing. Images appear, but I'm not sure what they are. It takes several seconds for me to realize the camera is focused in tightly and sweeping across parts of a car. A bumper, the tire, a dashboard, a door handle.

"A car," I say. "What is that supposed to mean?"

"I don't know," Sam says. The music gets slightly louder. "What is that music?"

I shake my head. "I'm not sure." The video ends, and Sam starts it again. On the third play-through, something strikes me as familiar. "Wait. Play that section again." Sam goes back slightly and replays the music. I hum along to it. "It sounds like the music played at an old movie. Let's all go to the lobby…"

He listens to me try to sing the jingle along with the video and nods.

"That's exactly what it is. So… the movie theater?"

"I don't know. That's too simple. It's showing a car."

"A drive-in?" he asks.

"Does Sherwood even have a drive-in?" I ask. "I don't remember there being one."

"It used to. Right outside town. It closed down a long time ago, but it's still there," he says.

"Let's go," I tell him.

"It might not be so easy," he says. "It's still there, but it's not just an abandoned drive-in."

"What is it?" I ask.

"A scrapyard."

CHAPTER TWENTY-FOUR

The screen is still here. It rises up at the end of the massive field, still stretched on its frame like at any moment the projector will kick on, and a film will play. Part of me waits for that to happen, for this whole thing to turn into a horror movie and the screen to start showing the gruesome final moments of one of the missing children. But the screen stays still and blank, and I can turn my attention to the sea of cars spread across the field.

The clamshell ramps of the original design of the drive-in are still evident; only now, the cars filling them are in various stages of damage, decay, and neglect. In some spots, several cars are stacked on top of each other, in a tenuous, tipping balance that threatens to topple at any second. In others, adrenaline-fueled teenage sprees have left windshields smashed in and pieces of trim scattered on the ground. My breath rattles in my chest.

"How are we supposed to know which car it is?" I ask. "There are thousands."

"We just have to start looking," Sam says. "That's all we can do."

He turns to the cars of search party members and officers who heeded his call to come to the old drive-In. People spill out, armed with bottles of water, flashlights, and long sticks. Some put on rugged work gloves and secure them around their wrists with Velcro straps. They're preparing to dismantle the tangled carcasses of the vehicles to search for whatever was left for us by hand.

Another car skids into place, diagonally blocking the way of one of the squad cars. Before the engine is completely silent, the door opens, and Caleb's mother jumps out. Her feet touch the ground in a full run as she descends the small hill toward Sam and me.

"Where is he?" she screams. "Where's my baby?"

"Kendra, you need to calm down," Sam says, holding up his hands to stop her progress.

"Don't tell me to calm down. I heard you were out here searching. You're searching for Caleb. You're searching for my baby."

"We don't know what we're searching for right now," I try to tell her. "The tip we got didn't provide any information. We don't even know for sure anything is out here."

"You don't really believe that. You found that little girl. Did you get a tip about that, too?" Kendra demands.

Her lips tremble, but she stiffens her jaw against the anger. Tears slide down her cheeks unchecked, and her dark eyes look fierce and wild.

"Please. We need to get the search started. Go home where you'll be comfortable out of this heat, and we will get in touch with you if there are any developments," Sam says.

"I'm not going anywhere. If my baby boy is out there somewhere in one of those cars, he's hot, too. I'm going to be right here."

"Fine. But you need to stay up here. I'll have an officer stay with you. I'm serious now, Kendra. Listen to me on this. You can't come down there and interfere. You need to stay here and be patient. This area is officially an active investigation."

She nods, relenting to the tenuous compromise, and Sam asks an officer named Samantha to stay with her. Someone in the search party has already set up a portable canopy and two large coolers full of ice and bottled water to create a makeshift cooling station. With the late afternoon sunlight radiating off the acres of metal and glass, I have a feeling we're going to need it.

Sam organizes all those available as a search and sends them in small groups up and down the rows of cars. Letting everyone wander into the rows without some sort of plan would waste time and energy, and risk missing the one car we're looking for. The methodical search of every car seems to crawl, but the slow pace means not worrying about missing something. But after almost an hour, a more intense worry starts to creep up inside me. I take Sam to the side.

"We can't keep moving this slowly," I tell him.

"If we move any faster, we might miss something," he says.

"I know. But if we keep moving this slowly, there's not going to be a single shred of a chance Caleb will survive."

"You really think this guy has Caleb out here?"

"I think it's the only thing that makes sense. He took them according to the alphabet; now he's eliminating them in the same way. And even if you discount the possibility of him still being alive, we can't just leave him out here. It's too hot, and the sun is too intense for these people to stay out here for long. We need to hurry."

"How? What are we supposed to do to move any faster?" he asks. "The video on the flash drive didn't tell us anything, not even the color of the paint."

I think about it for a second; then my eyes snap back to him.

"Maybe it did. Just not the way you're thinking. Did you bring it with us? With the envelope and everything?" I ask.

"It's in the car."

"Do you have a pen?"

"There should be one in the glove compartment. What are you doing?"

"Maybe nothing. But let's see just how tricky this guy can be," I say.

Going back to Sam's car, I get inside and pick up the envelope. I pull the paper out of it and reach into the glove compartment for a pen. Spreading the paper out on my lap, I look it over.

"The newspaper the flash drive was wrapped in?" Sam asks.

I shake my head. "No. Well, yes, but not exactly. This is newsprint, but the crossword isn't from a newspaper. It was printed on there separately with a regular printer. See where the edge of the puzzle smeared slightly? That's why there aren't any articles or anything else. Those don't matter. This puzzle is what he wanted us to see. If we were able to find it. We just have to figure out what it's hiding."

"One across. Home of Hawthorne. House of the blank Gables," Sam reads.

"Seven," I say, filling out the blocks. "Sixteen down, Biblical prophet and kingmaker. Six letters." My eyes lift sharply to his.

"Samuel," he frowns.

"What do you think the chances are that that's a coincidence?" I ask.

"Nothing. Keep going."

"Three across. Topic of the first book published in the American colonies."

We look at each other, and he pulls out his phone.

"Psalms."

We keep working, filling in the blocks. We're moving through the puzzle as fast as we can, but it feels like every second is longer than the last. Around us, I hear the sounds of metal grinding against metal and car doors slamming. Red-faced people come to the cooling shelter to drain bottles of water and slide ice down their shirts. They're fading, but I can't let them stop. Not yet.

"Eleven across. Spy sent to find the land of Canaan," I murmur. I gasp and jump to my feet. "Caleb. Eleven across. It's eleven across. Find the eleventh row."

Sam and I look out over the cars and start running toward the eleventh row.

"Which one?" he asks. "There are hundreds of cars in this row."

Searchers from around us have heard the commotion and run up to the row. They're scrambling over the cars, tearing open doors and popping trunks. Caleb's name reverberates through the air, louder than the sound of the metal. I look back at the puzzle and the blocks where his name fills the clue. It borrows the 'C' from another answer, and I check the number of that clue.

"Twenty-seven," I say. "The 'C' of his name is in twenty-seven down."

Sam starts counting off the cars as we run down the row. My eyes hit the car before he gets to it. I recognize the bumper from the video. A tell-tale dent in the back corner sets it apart. The first place I go is the trunk. I brace myself as it pops open, but there's nothing inside but a tire iron and an empty oil bottle. Sam gets to the car and opens the back seats. He tears out a blanket and starts pulling up the cushions.

"Nothing," he says. "He's not here." He pulls back and lunges forward, slamming himself against the side of the car. "Fuck!"

The car rocks to the side, and both of us take a step back. It shouldn't have moved that much. Sam is strong, but not powerful enough to shift a massive vehicle that easily. I run to the front and yank up on the hood.

The engine of a car weighs just over three hundred pounds. The weight of a broken, balled-up eleven-year-old boy doesn't anchor it in the same way.

Kendra should have listened to Sam. She shouldn't have broken away from Samantha's grip and run to join the group gathered around the car. Her primal, soul-tearing scream will stay with me for a long, long time.

CHAPTER TWENTY-FIVE

"Call 911!" someone screams as Sam climbs over the hood of a car wedged up beside the front corner of this one.

I scramble after him and look down under the hood. The car has been gutted, and where the engine should be sitting is a cage that hangs almost like a basket from hooks attached to either side of the car. The cage is so shallow the metal grate of the top sits down on Caleb's side, pressing into the skin of his arm and leg, and crushing against his hip. A row of zip ties set at intervals of only a few centimeters around the entire perimeter secures the cage closed.

"Does anyone have strong scissors or small wire cutters?" I ask.

"I have a knife," the man beside me offers.

"That will do. Thank you."

I take the knife from him and tuck the blade under one of the zip ties. It strains against the plastic, but eventually cracks through and pops it open. Sam takes pictures of the area and the cage as I continue around the edge. When he steps back, someone else from the crowd rushes up with a pair of bolt cutters.

"Emma, step back," Sam says, taking the tool.

"You have to be careful," I tell him. "The metal is right against his skin. You can't just cut the links."

"Hold it up," he instructs.

I tuck my fingers into the gaps of the chain link and pull up with as much strength as I can. Grateful for my height and the leverage it gives me, I manage to create a small gap between the metal and Caleb. It's not much room, but it's enough to provide some protection as Sam uses the blades to cut through several of the zip ties at one time.

Kendra forces her way through the crowd again and comes up beside me. I feel her body shaking as she stares blankly at her son like her mind has closed down, and she's no longer processing what she's seeing.

The top of the cage finally opens, and Sam pushes it back. He and another man reach in to take hold of Caleb and start lifting him out. The limited space makes the movement awkward, and they struggle with his dead weight. I reach forward and open my arms, encouraging Sam to drape the boy in them. Glancing over my shoulder, I meet eyes with Kendra.

"I need you to help me," I tell her. The wail of the ambulance siren finally sounds in the distance, and I look at her more intensely. "Hear that? They're coming. They're on their way. But we need to get him out. Take your son."

She finally seems to hear me and steps up closer so I can maneuver Caleb from Sam's arms across the corner of the car and into his mother's arms. She holds him to her chest and sinks down onto the ground, cradling him like a baby and sobbing into his shoulder.

"Is he alive?" I ask Sam softly.

"I don't know."

I don't remember getting back to my house last night. Or very early this morning, depending on how you look at it. We were at the scrapyard for hours after finding Caleb, then had to go back to the station for interviews, paperwork, and processing more evidence. At some point in the predawn darkness Sam brought me back to the house. I only made it as far as the living room couch. I'm still in my clothes, and the gritty feeling of dried sweat and dirt clings to my skin. A hot shower cuts through the feeling and the fog, so by the time I get out, I'm human again.

Sam is at my door before I'm finished with my first cup of coffee, but he has a travel cup for me, and I gulp it gratefully as we head out in silence. Neither of us are looking forward to where we're going, but it's what has to be done. I'm doing my best to control my anger, and I can tell he is as well, though I think he has a better chance of doing it than I do. He's always been more even, better able to take hold of his emotions and manage them even in the most difficult situations. Last night on our way to the station when we made the plan for this morning, we promised each other and ourselves, we'd keep it together.

The car behind us follows at just enough distance to give us time to get inside a short time before they pull up. It will hopefully make this smoother.

When we get to Vincent's house, my first instinct is to check the driveway and see how many cars are sitting there. The fact that there's two takes the thought of this going at all smoothly out of my mind.

"Valerie's here," I tell Sam.

"She's going to be fine," he says.

"She's going to pitch a fucking fit," I mutter.

"She's going to have to deal with this. She doesn't have a choice."

Vincent doesn't look surprised when he opens the door to us standing on his porch.

"Sheriff, Emma. I thought you'd be coming this morning."

"Since you ran away from us before we could talk to you at the scrapyard last night, I think it was a pretty safe bet," Sam says.

"I was there in an official capacity. I had my press pass," he defends himself.

"Your press pass means absolutely nothing in a situation like this," I say.

"Vincent, you are too close to this to be reporting on it. The clues are coming to you and... "

149

"And that means I have a responsibility to report what's happening," he says.

"You have a responsibility to keep people as safe as possible and support the department in the investigation," I point out.

"What if that's what I'm doing? Whoever this is chose me to send the envelopes to. You're the one who said that. He chose me."

"Vincent, we need an explanation. Something we can go on," Sam says.

"What do you mean?" Vincent asks.

"Twice now you've claimed to have found anonymous packages on your front porch with strange messages inside. And both times, those messages have led directly to one of the missing children. There has to be more to it than that," Sam tells him.

Vincent looks back and forth between us, his eyes growing wider and more desperate.

"You think it was me? I swear, I didn't have anything to do with those kids. I could never hurt a child."

The other car pulls up in front of the house, and an investigative team steps out with their equipment.

"I'm sorry, Vincent," Sam sighs. "I don't like this, and I don't want to do it, but I would be failing in my duties if I didn't. As of right now, you are under investigation. A search warrant for your house is on its way. Are you going to make us wait for it to get here to let us in?"

Vincent shakes his head. "No. Do whatever you need to do."

"Thank you."

We follow him into the house, and he stands in the middle of the entryway while the other officers come inside. Sam gives instructions in a quiet voice, trying to keep the situation as calm as possible. The control lasts only a few seconds. Valerie's footsteps coming down the stairs are enough to shake the house. Her eyes alight with fury when she sees us.

"What are you doing here?" she asks. "How many times do I have to tell you not to come onto my property and harass my family?"

"We're not harassing him," I say.

"They're investigating me," Vincent tells her.

"What?" Valerie gasps. "You have to be kidding."

"I wish I was," I say.

"This is beyond ridiculous. Can't you see how much damage you're causing? I don't feel safe in my own home. Singer can't even spend time with his friends because neighbors have seen you people here so much and are taunting him about it. But even worse, you're wasting time you should be spending on the investigation. While you're here digging through my house, you could be focusing on finding the person who actually did this."

"Valerie, it's going to be alright," Vincent says. "They need to do what they need to do."

"They need to do what they need to do?" she repeats incredulously. "They are putting the rest of the children of Sherwood, including our son, in more danger by not getting this guy off the street."

"That's what we're trying to do," Sam says. "We need to follow every lead possible and start eliminating possibilities. For now, you need to step aside so we can finish what we're doing."

"No. I'm not going to let you ravage my home," she says.

"We're not ravaging anything. We're searching. And you don't have a choice. Either you stop impeding our search and let us do our job, or I arrest you for interfering with an investigation, and you can sit at the jail until we're done. It's up to you."

"Fine. We have nothing to hide. Get this over with so you can stop bothering us and let us have our lives back."

She steps back and watches through angry, narrowed eyes as the team gathers stacks of notebooks, papers, books, and computers to bring out. Maybe somewhere in all that, we will find something. And if not, it will let us close that path and start on a new one.

CHAPTER TWENTY-SIX

Rather than heading back to the station after we leave Vincent's house, Sam turns in the opposite direction.

"Where are we going?" I ask. "I thought you would want to start looking through that evidence as soon as possible."

"I do," he says, "but there's somewhere we need to go first."

"Where?

"The community center."

In all the chaos of the flash drive and the search through the scrapyard, I didn't even remember the fourth child to go missing. Now it crashes back down on me, and my mind starts churning. Now there are two still missing. Two we can't account for.

We get to the other side of town, and Sam pulls the car into the parking lot outside the large church I remember in scattered memories. When I was much younger, my grandparents came to services every week and often brought me along with them. As I get older in my mind, the memories become fewer. Most of them revolve around the social events rather than the services themselves. Out of the corner of my eye, I see Sam glance my way. I know he remembers the Valentine's Day dance and the summer picnic, too.

"What are we doing here?" I ask. "I thought we were going to the community center."

"We are," he nods, climbing out of the car. "It's attached to the church."

"It is?"

"A lot has stayed the same around here since you were gone, but there've been some changes, too."

We walk through the parking lot and up the sidewalk like we're going to head into the main portion of the building where the sanctuary is, but then Sam turns. He leads me around the side of the building toward what I remember was a small playground and field of scrub grass. Now a large addition sits out from the main church, hidden from view from the parking lot, but sprawling once we get to the end of the sidewalk. Where the small playground once had just enough swings for children to get very good at taking turns and a slide that made waste of many a Sunday dress, new, elaborate equipment sprouts up from rubber mulch.

"This is definitely new," I comment.

Sam nods. "The community wanted a place where people could come together and feel connected. The adult and continuing education people had been wanting to get out of the high school for a long time. And since Sarah, the lady who used to run one of the daycares in town, shut hers down, parents needed somewhere they could trust to leave their children. The community center was born of all that. The church had additional funding in their budget, and the land, and we ran a few big fundraisers, and here we are now."

"It's really nice."

He holds the door open for me, and I walk into the sharply cold air conditioning inside the community center. A curved blue reception desk sits at an angle in the small lobby area, and a pretty blonde woman smiles at us over the cover of a well-loved paperback. She holds it up and gives a grin and half-shrug.

"I know I'm supposed to be clamoring for a tablet and evangelizing the virtues of the ebook, but I can't help it. I like pages."

"Me, too," I tell her.

"Is there some sort of art program for children going on here this week?" Sam asks.

The woman nods cheerfully. "You bet. The young ones do seem to enjoy it. It's amazing what they can create when their little minds are just allowed to go."

"It is," he agrees. "Can you point me in the direction of where that's held?"

Her eyes suddenly darken, and the smile fades from her lips.

"Oh, no. Is this about Gloria? I hoped her mother would have figured out what happened by now."

"Can you show me where the room is?" Sam asks again, not giving anything away.

The woman points to one hallway leading away from the lobby and gives us a simple set of instructions.

"I forgot how fast news travels around here," I say as we make our way to the large open room. Inside several tables are packed with children, while others take up sections of the floor and activity centers set up around the room. To one side, the walls extend out to create an office. I notice a clipboard hanging from the wall just inside the door. "Here's the sign-out sheet Bianca was talking about."

Sam flips the top page back and runs his finger down the list. "And there's Bianca's signature saying she picked Gloria up."

I take the several steps to the side it takes to get away from the door to the office and back to a position overlooking the room full of children.

"The way the office is set up, you can't see the door or the clipboard from most of the room," I point out. "Unless someone was in the office or specifically watching for it, it's likely no one would see a parent signing their child out."

"Good afternoon, Sheriff," a woman says, walking up to us and eyeing the clipboard in my hands. "Is there something I can help you with?"

"Yes. I need to talk to whoever is in charge of the art program," he says.

155

"That's me. I'm Holly Devlin." She shakes his hand. "I run this program and a few of the others at the community center."

"Are you here every day?" I ask.

"Yes. As you can probably imagine, community centers don't usually enjoy the luxury of a big staff. I love these programs and want them to be the best they can possibly be for the children and the rest of the community, so I am here every day the center is open. Six days a week. Usually from opening until close."

"So, you were here when Bianca Hernandez came to pick up her daughter and realized she was missing," Sam says.

Holly's back stiffens, and she pulls her shoulders back almost protectively.

"Yes. It was a particularly busy day, and the children were more restless than usual because we didn't go outside for as long as we normally do. The weather wasn't good, and I didn't think they should be out there. One of the girls who assists me got sick and had to go home early, so things were a little chaotic. I knew Gloria was going to be leaving early. Her mother let me know at the beginning of the day that she was only working part of the day and would be by to get Gloria in the early afternoon. I hoped to see her off, but a group of boys got into a scuffle, and while I was handling it, she left."

"So, you didn't see her leave or see Bianca?" I ask.

"No. I was in the back corner of the room at the clay table. I can't see the office or the sign-out sheet from there. When I was done handling the situation with the boys, I noticed Gloria was no longer in the room. A few of the others said she took her stuff and left, so I went and checked the sheet. Bianca had signed her out," Holly says.

"And you're sure this is her signature?" I ask, pointing to the clipboard.

Holly nods. "You can look back through the sheets from the other days, and I have some on record from other activities and events she has attended." I nod, and she leads us into the office where she pulls out a file folder and hands me a stack of sheets.

"I keep every sign-out sheet used in the center for a year. There have been occasions where we've been asked by the courts to prove a child attends certain programs or was in the center at a certain time, or to show the reliability of a parent. And there are times when I bring these out at budget meetings to show proof of how many children attend certain programs consistently. I like to keep verifiable records. I can say twenty children are here for the weekend yoga class as many times as I want, but the committee is much more compelled by looking at papers that show parents signing their children out on a regular basis. It shows that they were there and stayed through the entire program."

I look over several of the sheets and compare Bianca's signatures.

"They aren't the same. I mean, no one signs things the exact same way every time, but there are some of these that look... odd. The letters are a little shaky or look like she was pressing really hard into the paper. That doesn't necessarily mean anything. She could have been stressed or tired those days. Both of those can change the way handwriting looks."

Sam and Holly exchange glances, each looking at the other like they know a secret and are wondering if the other does, too.

"Have you had any interactions with Bianca recently?" he asks her.

It means something more than just the words.

"I spoke to her briefly two days before Gloria went missing," she tells him.

"How was she?"

"She seemed... distracted. But there was nothing I could do. Without any evidence of anything going on, I had no choice but to let her take her daughter," Holly says.

"Evidence of what?" I ask.

Sam looks at me with a pained expression.

"Bianca has had some issues with alcohol," he says. "It's a problem in her entire family, so she has some genetic predisposition to it, and the stress of being a single mother and dealing with her ex pushes her over the edge sometimes. She was getting much better, but..."

"But maybe she doesn't remember coming to pick Gloria up

because she blacked out. Or maybe she did something to her, and she doesn't actually have anything to do with the other missing children at all," I say.

He stares back at me, and I give a single nod. "Good to know." I look at Holly. "Thank you for your time. You've been very helpful."

CHAPTER TWENTY-SEVEN

S am says a few more words to Holly before following me out, but I don't care what they are. I just want to be out of that place. He finally calls out to me when I'm almost at the car, and I spin around to look at him.

"What's wrong?" he asks.

"Why didn't you tell me?" I ask.

"I should have. I'm sorry."

"That's not what I asked. Why didn't you tell me the mother of a missing child whose disappearance we're investigating, who also happens to be your ex-girlfriend, has a history of a serious drinking problem?"

"Which part bothers you worse, the mother of the missing child or the fact that she's my ex?" he asks.

"Don't try to get cute with me right now, Sam. This could completely change everything about our investigation. You should know that. Why didn't you tell me the truth?" I ask.

"It's not something she wants a lot of people to know," he tells me.

"The woman who works at the community center apparently knows," I say.

"She knows because Bianca had to go to treatment. In order for

Gloria to continue going to the programs at the community center, Bianca had to show she was managing her condition appropriately and making progress. Holly is supposed to help hold her accountable."

"Apparently, she's not doing that great of a job."

"She can't be with Bianca every single second of her life. She's not a doctor or a counselor," he says. "Bianca has to learn to do it for herself."

"And if she doesn't? The point is, we jumped right into this situation under the assumption Gloria is another victim of this murderer. But if Bianca was drunk when she came to pick her up, she could have hurt her or done something with her, then gone back to try to cover her tracks acting like she was just coming to pick her up for the first time, not remembering she signed the sheet. This could be a completely different thing."

"Let me call her, and we'll ask her a few questions," he offers.

Ten tense and silent minutes later, Bianca pulls up beside the car and steps out.

"That was fast," Sam says.

"I didn't take my lunch yet. What's going on? Are you here about Gloria?" Her hands come up to cover her mouth as her eyes widen and fill with tears. "Oh, no. Did something happen to her?"

Sam reaches out to touch her arm and calm her.

"We don't know anything yet," he says. "We just came here to talk to Holly to see if we could get any additional details. And we wanted to look at the sign-out sheet."

"Did you see it? It looks like my handwriting, doesn't it?" she asks.

"We did see it. And it does look like your handwriting. Sometimes."

Her eyes flicker back and forth between us with uncertainty.

"What do you mean sometimes?" she asks.

"We got a chance to look back through the last several months of sheets and compare your signatures on each. There are a few times where it varies kind of wildly. But other parts of it show you really did write it."

He pauses, as if he's trying to give her the chance to just come out and tell him what's going on, but she keeps staring at him, waiting for him to go on. "Holly says you've been drinking again."

Bianca recoils. Her expression is stung, like Sam hit her.

"She told you that?" she asks, her voice softer now.

"Yes. She's worried, Bianca. She thinks it's possible you did come and get Gloria, but then you forgot that you signed her out."

"Are you blaming me? My daughter is missing, and you're trying to say it's my fault because I drink?"

"Not because you drink, but because you have a drinking problem," I say.

She looks me up and down with disgust. "Where do you come off judging me? Whether or not I drink is none of your business."

"Actually, it is," I tell her. "Considering I'm currently assisting with the investigation into the abductions of several children, including yours, it's the very definition of my business. Right now, we have nothing to go on when it comes to your daughter. No one saw her leave, and there are no cameras recording the community center or the church. I would think members of the staff here who have seen you many times before and know you are connected to Gloria would recognize if a stranger came into the building and left with her."

"Are you accusing me of something?" Bianca asks.

"I'm not accusing. I'm stating observations and facts. If there's any chance something else could have happened to Gloria that doesn't have anything to do with the other missing children, time is being wasted. You need to be honest with us."

"How dare you? Sam, are you going to let her talk to me like that?"

"Bianca…" he starts.

Her eyes widen as she realizes he's not going to jump to her defense.

"I trusted you. I thought you cared about Gloria."

"I do," he tells her.

"Just not enough to leave the past in the past. I guess once you get an FBI bitch sniffing around after you, it's easy to just throw other people away."

She climbs back into her car. Her wheels screech as she drives out of the parking lot to disappear away from the church. I let out a breath.

"I'm sorry she said that. And that I wasn't upfront with you from the beginning," he says to me.

I shake my head. "She doesn't bother me. I've been called worse. A lot worse. Now, the comment about me sniffing around after you I could have done without."

I snicker, and Sam relaxes slightly. "You know you are. You've always been so impressed by me." He smiles and heads for the car. "Come on."

My gaze moves over to the front entrance of the church.

"Actually, let's go inside."

"Why do you want to go in the church? Are you having a nostalgic moment?" he asks.

"Not exactly. Let's just say I think we might benefit from a little bit of spiritual guidance."

We walk into the church, and it immediately hits me that it smells the exact same. Churches hold onto the impressions of moments, much like crime scenes do. You can walk through them and feel what has happened long before you were there. The church building is silent, but every step radiates with the energy of the countless people and life moments that have touched this space. Assuming the layout of the building hasn't undergone any drastic changes since the last time I was here, I follow the path of the hallways by memory to end up at the door to the pastor's office.

"What are we doing here?" Sam asks.

"I just want to talk to Pastor Robins for a minute," I tell him.

Before Sam can protest, I knock on the door. The pastor opens it, looking more casual with his shirt rolled up to his elbows, and his tie loosened slightly.

"Hello," he says.

"Pastor, my name is Emma Griffin."

"Yes, Ms. Griffin. I know who you are. I've been following the news pretty closely. Is there something I can do for you?"

"I just had a few things I wanted to ask you. As the spiritual leader for much of Sherwood, you might have some insights that could prove helpful," I say.

"I'm not sure if I can be of any help, but I'll certainly try. Come on in." Sam and I follow him into the office and wait while he clears his desk of papers that were spread across it. "I'm sorry. I was just going over some counseling exercises. Just give me one second." He sets the papers aside and sits down. "Alright. What would you like to know?"

"Did you know Alice Brooks well?" I ask.

I watch how his face reacts to hearing her name, but don't notice any major changes.

"Yes. Her mother does a lot of volunteer work around the church, and I got familiar with Alice when she would come in with Ms. Brooks."

"So, you would know if she was an impulsive child? The type of child who might just walk off in the middle of the night or follow a dare from other children?" I ask.

"I wouldn't describe her as impulsive. She was a very quiet child, shy and usually very content to just be with her mother or even by herself with her books."

"Usually?"

"She seemed to me like she was starting to grow up a little and was looking for some independence and friends, but maybe wasn't ready to say that for herself. That's why Ms. Brooks sent her to camp. She wanted to help her break out of her shell a little more," the pastor explains.

"So, she might have enjoyed the newfound freedom and been compelled to do something out of character."

"Possibly."

"And what about Caleb Donahue? His mother tells us he and your son became good friends over the last couple of months. Did you notice anything about him that was unusual the day he left your house?" I ask.

He pauses for slightly longer after that question, but still seems unfazed.

"No. He was the same active, happy boy he always was when he came over. The boys camped out in the living room the night before, then that day hung out inside for the morning. They were throwing a baseball around when Caleb said it was time to head home."

"And he walked?" I ask.

"We don't live very far away from the Donahue's neighborhood, and I was under the impression he was getting picked up a few blocks away."

"By one of his family members?"

"That would be my guess. It happened several times before."

"And Eva. She was supposed to go on a youth group trip the morning she disappeared, is that right?" I ask.

He nods. "Yes. I lead the youth group for her age, and we were planning a day trip to a nearby park for some swimming and water-slides. It was a celebration for them finishing a volunteer project they had been working on for several months. She was very excited about it."

"As the leader of the youth group, does that mean you were driving the van that was supposed to pick her up?"

"Yes. I drive for all of the youth group activities. I arrived at her grandparents' house at exactly the appointed time, but she didn't come out. I had already picked up a few of the other children and couldn't leave them unattended in the car, so I beeped the horn for her. But she wasn't there."

"What did you do?"

"I called her grandparents to find out if there was a change in plans or if she was somewhere else. They rushed home from work, and I took the rest of the children on their trip," he says.

"The same question as with Alice. Did Eva seem impulsive? Or prone to make poor decisions?"

"Not at all," he insists. "She thrived under her grandparents' care. She was always extremely well behaved and polite. She followed the rules, was respectful. Even when the other children acted up, as they sometimes do because they're children, she didn't go along with it. That's why it's so surprising she would go against the plans we made."

"Interesting." I stand up and smile at the pastor. "Well, thank you very much for your time. I won't keep you any longer."

"Absolutely. I hope I was of some help to you."

He reaches for the papers again, and I point at them. "Did you say you were going over counseling exercises? I actually just started getting very interested in self-improvement through counseling."

"It's always good to see someone willing to do the work to achieve their best self. These exercises aren't personal use, though. I do some spiritually-based counseling for couples, and this is a favorite exercise of mine to help them communicate more effectively. People often feel vulnerable when they are expected to express themselves face to face. Writing each other letters helps them to open up and think through what they want the other to know. It gives some time for them to really think about what their partner told them and what they want to say in return. It can make some extraordinary progress in couples struggling to connect and encourage those just starting out to create a strong foundation in their relationship."

"Maybe I'll work on writing letters to myself," I say.

"I think that's just journaling, Ms. Griffin. But I highly recommend that, too. It's always good to get your feelings out when you don't have to worry about what someone else is going to think or say."

"Have a good day, Pastor," I say.

"You, too." I start out of the room, but his voice stops me. "I meant to ask. Have you reached out to Eva Francis's father?"

"Her father?" I ask, turning around to look at him again. "He's in jail."

"No," the pastor says, shaking his head. "He came by the church about three weeks ago asking about his parents and Eva."

CHAPTER TWENTY-EIGHT

"How could Janet and Paul not tell us their son was out of jail?" I ask. "Does no one tell the truth anymore?"

I stalk through the parking lot and toss myself into the passenger seat. Sam gets in beside me and cranks the engine.

"It's possible they don't know," he offers.

"How could they not know?"

"They had to deal with all the trouble he has caused and worry about their granddaughter. Do you really think he doesn't know how worried his parents would be if they knew he was back out and looking for his daughter? They adore that little girl, and they've obviously been doing a fantastic job raising her. They wouldn't do anything to put her at risk. If he was out, they would do everything they could to protect Eva," he says. "If that really was Eva's father who came here looking for her, his parents don't know he's out."

"Then we need to find him."

We drive out of the parking lot, and Sam looks over at me.

"Why did you want to go talk to the pastor?" he asks, a slightly prying note in his voice.

"I told you. Spiritual guidance."

"There's one more place I want to stop before we go to the station."

"Sure. Hopefully that means by the time we get there, they'll be done processing everything into custody, and we can dig in," I say.

It doesn't take long for us to get to our next destination. We park and walk through huge glass sliding doors into a marble-floored room. To one side, an art installation looks like a waterfall with a constant stream running down between two panes of glass. Sam hits the button for the elevator, and I take a breath as we glide up through the floors of the building. The doors open to a large, quiet network of hallways and rooms. A woman looks up at us from a desk and gives a slight smile. We walk past the desk and along two hallways to get to a partially closed door at the end. Sam knocks on it lightly, then pushes it open so we can step inside.

Kendra Donahue looks up at us from the side of the bed. She looks like she's been sitting there without moving since yesterday.

"Can we come in?" Sam asks.

She nods and wipes tears away from her cheeks. Her other hand rests on the bed, turned up, so Caleb's rests in her palm. An IV taped to his skin pumps fluids continuously through him, while tubes in his nostrils deliver oxygen to help his damaged lungs. He looks so small in the bed, a handmade blanket that looks heavily loved draped over him. But his chest is moving. Rising and falling. Each breath separating him from the brink he hovered on less than twenty-four hours ago.

"How is he?" I ask.

Kendra nods, looking down at him and stroking her thumb across the back of his hand.

"Doing better. He still hasn't woken up, but the doctors say they expect that soon. He got so overheated his body shut down. It needs the rest to repair itself. They're planning on doing some scans later to check for any brain damage."

"Good," I say.

She sets her son's hand down gently and stands up.

"I don't know what to say."

"You don't have to say anything," Sam tells her.

"I do. Just thank you. Thank you so much for finding him. You saved my baby. The doctors say the cage being suspended in the car like that gave it enough air circulation to help him last longer. But even still, he wouldn't have lasted for much longer if you hadn't found him. If it wasn't for you, he would still be out there in that car."

"But he's not," I tell her. "He's here. And he'll pull through. He's a strong boy."

Kendra gathers me in a hug, and I give it back, for the first time since seeing Caleb curled up in that horrible little cage, his skin wet with sweat and his body limp, really feeling relief.

"Have you found out anything?" she asks as she steps back.

"Not yet," Sam tells her.

"But we're working on it. We won't stop until we get him. Just trust us," I say.

"I do."

She goes and sits back down, picking up Caleb's hand and kissing it. He's not out of the woods yet. We don't know how long he was in that engine compartment or what might have happened to him before he was put there. The damage done to his brain and body could be extensive, and the doctors won't really know the full extent until they do scans, and he wakes up. All anyone can do now is wait.

B y the time we get to the station and wait while the evidence taken from Vincent's house is boxed, I don't want to sit around here anymore. It feels like eyes are constantly on me, waiting for my next move, and I want to get away from it. Taking the boxes of notebooks and papers with us, Sam and I go back to my house. A few things have changed since I got here. I've taken down some of the art put up by the management company and shifted the arrangement of the furniture in a couple of the rooms. The kitchen cabinets are full, and the house now smells like coffee and soap and life.

"Are you hungry?" Sam asks as he sets down one of the crates in the living room.

This has been the one room we've occupied together other than briefly in the kitchen. It's easy stepping right into the house and turning into this room, letting us almost create a neutral space.

"No," I tell him.

"You have to eat something. I haven't seen you eat at all today. How about I order a pizza? Graziano's is still open."

"Meatball and onions?" I ask.

"Would I order anything else?"

I relent to the memories. Nothing compares to the pizza Sam and I used to eat together when we were younger. I've spent my adult years longing for it and trying to find something, anything that comes anywhere close. But I've never been able to.

"What should we look through first?" I ask, kicking off my shoes and folding myself into the corner of the couch. "There's a lot here."

"I don't even know what we're looking for," he says.

"Anything. If Vincent really is creating those clues himself, there might be something in these to prove it. Even when things seem like they are so carefully thought out, people tend to make really ridiculous mistakes. They plan taking a hostage for three years, but then leave a receipt sitting on the counter that has the rope and plastic container right there on it. Sometimes when someone goes through the effort of being elaborate and complex, they miss the simplest of details. It's just our job to find it."

"Inspiring," Sam says, taking the chair positioned diagonally from me and taking a stack into his lap.

After an hour of reading through the first few notebooks, I reach for a new folder, then look at Sam.

"Do you have anything over there in Valerie's handwriting?" I ask.

"Um," he looks at his lap and at the papers strewn across it and the table in front of him. "Yes. Here."

I take the paper he holds out to me and look down at it.

"It's a grocery list," I tell him.

"You didn't specify what you wanted in her handwriting, just that you wanted her handwriting," he says.

"I need something with more substance."

"I have a book with an inscription, though I find 'milk, eggs, aluminum foil, apple sauce' a pretty meaningful slam poetry type thing if you really search for the depth behind it."

He offers the book out to me, and I take it from his hand with a shake of my head.

"You need more sleep. Just going to put that out there," I say.

"Yeah. I'll be sure to check right back in with you when that happens," he says.

I open the cover of the book and look at the inscription. The handwriting is smooth and seamless.

"This is exactly what I would think her handwriting would look like," I say.

"Really? It's so perfect, and she's so…"

"On edge?"

"Yeah," he says.

"Yeah. That's pretty common, actually. You would think the really high-strung people would have really chaotic handwriting, but they usually don't. It's almost unnervingly controlled. Look at Vincent's writing." I hold one of the notebooks out for him to see. "There are variations in it. It's pretty consistent, but there are some changes in the size of the letters or the spacing of the words. Sometimes it's obviously rushed and messier. But Valerie strives for more control than that. She has to project a certain image and make sure other people see her that way."

"So, you don't think she really cares if we're giving Vincent a bad rep. It's that it's her husband, and she wants her family to maintain the right image," he says.

I shrug. "It's a possibility. I don't see a lot of love between the two of them. Not to say they dislike each other or anything, but there just isn't that warmth."

"Again, that's just Valerie. Warm is not a word I'd use to describe her. She can be friendly and pleasant, but she's never going to be the woman you drink hot tea with and talk about your problems."

"Do you do that frequently with women?" I ask.

He laughs. "Not often."

I look back at the notebook in my hand and flip through a few pages. "It looks like we might need to find Vincent someone to have hot tea with. He has a lot of emotions going on here." I look at another notebook, then a stack of papers. "A whole lot. Have you noticed almost none of this stuff is Valerie's? It's all Vincent. With the way you talked about her loving to read, I really thought I was going to find journals or notes or something from her. Instead, all these notebooks seem to be Vincent waxing poetic about life. He goes on these long monologues; then there'll be a few pages of just random thoughts."

"What do you think are the chances he's writing a novel?" Sam asks.

"It's possible. These might just be ideas he's jotting down or dreams he's had. But there are things in here that sound like he's addressing something specific. He talks about wondering what love really is and if it can exist without longing. He wonders why she can't give him the love he's craving and if it will ever be possible for her to be what he wants her to be."

"Damn. Harsh," Sam comments.

"It really is. I was feeling really bad for him because of the rumors about Valerie's affair with Jennings, but this is changing my view a bit," I say. "Do you think that could be why she had the affair? She didn't feel like her husband loved her, or she wasn't good enough, so she fell for someone who did pay attention to her?"

"I really don't know. Like I said, it was years ago. If she was so unhappy, why would she still be with him?" he asks. "She could have just left him for Jennings."

"Maybe Vincent told her he would change, and they'd work on it, but it just never happened."

"Or she just couldn't stand the thought of other people seeing her as a divorcee," he suggests.

"That would be the type of image she wouldn't want to have. She needs the fairy tale, and none of the Disney princesses get alimony checks."

CHAPTER TWENTY-NINE

"What is your gut feeling about Vincent?" Sam asks.

"What do you mean?" I ask.

"We're scouring through all this trying to find something that links him to the clues or gives any indication he's behind all this happening. But all we've figured out so far is he writes down apparently every thought that goes through his mind."

"It's interesting you put it that way," I say.

"Why?"

"What's something that's distinctly missing from any of this stuff?"

"Consistent application of grammar rules?"

"Mentions of the missing children," I point out. "Now, we haven't read every single word in all these, but think about what you just said. We've just gone through pages and pages of him rambling about sometimes completely random thoughts. Things that contradict each other. Questions. Everything. He's a reporter. The compulsion to record what he's thinking and feeling is real; I understand that. That act helps him to distill what he's going through and process it more effectively. But if he's that compelled to write down everything he's thinking, and he's the one responsible for these children going missing, wouldn't there be something in here that suggests that? Wouldn't he mention the children or the clues?"

"He wouldn't want to write something down he didn't want other people to know about. If he's trying to make it look like someone else is doing these things, he wouldn't completely blow it by recording all the details," Sam points out.

"He didn't have reason to think anyone would ever see these but him. Do you honestly think he would write some of those things laying his soul out bare and admitting to those things if he thought there was a chance anyone else was going to be reading it? These are his personal thoughts. He would pour out his musings about the children just like he did all these other things. Think of it this way… why would he want to kidnap those children?" I ask. "What's the motivation?"

"Notoriety," Sam shrugs. "Remember, from the very beginning, he was planning on splashing this all over the news."

I nod. "He wants to be a famous reporter and known for his in-depth accounts of the most sensational news stories. But you said it yourself. Nothing like this happens in Sherwood. Jennings jumped ship and went somewhere else to chase the big news."

"So, Vincent decided to create his own major news story with him in the starring role as the recipient of mysterious clues that led inves-tigators to the bodies. Emma, you just gave Vincent motive. You cemented him as the prime suspect."

I shake my head. "No, I didn't. I proved he shouldn't be a suspect at all. If he wants all this attention and to be seen as an incredible reporter, he's going to plan everything out very carefully. This isn't something he can just throw together on a whim. He has to plan for which children he's going to take, what he's going to do with them, and the way he's going to present the clues. That's all really intensive thinking and planning. There's no way he'd go through all that without having to write something down. He would mention some-thing about the children, the kidnappings, the murder, or even the investigation. Even if he didn't say it straight out, he would do some-thing veiled with it. He'd do some sort of rambling analysis of it and work through what was going on in his mind. Especially after Caleb lived. But I've only found one thing. A question. 'Why did you have to tell the police?'"

"He's regretting telling us about the clues?" Sam frowns. "Why? They did what they were meant to do. They brought us to Alice and Caleb. We were even able to keep Caleb alive because we got there fast enough."

"But it's also calling attention to the problems in his marriage. It lured Jennings back into their lives. He might have reached a point where he believes the children's lives are a worthy sacrifice to try to keep piecing his marriage together. He never says he doesn't want to be with her or that he wants them to separate. He even talks about longing. If he has an idealized version in his mind of what love is supposed to be and how their marriage could be what it should be, he might be willing to just hope we have enough to go on and will stop this guy without his involvement."

A strange sound in the back of the house makes me stop. The hair stands up on the back of my neck as I listen. A steady, slow thump sounds like it's coming from the stairs. I stand up, and a sudden burst of flame shoots across the wall, crawling along the paint and igniting the room. Embers like droplets of rain fall down on the furniture and papers, sending them up immediately. In seconds, the room is engulfed. I scream and turn to Sam, but he's draped back across the chair, flames already consuming him.

I have to get out of the house. I move toward the front door, but a wall of flame stops me. It's blocking the door and the window along the front wall. My only choice is to go through the house to the back door. I run out of the room and get to the bottom of the stairs. The thumping sound is louder here, and something dark moves above me. I look up and see a blackened figure moving slowly down the steps. The flames are so bright they sear my vision and make it difficult for me to see, so I keep running. A loud crack overhead makes me step back an instant before a section of the ceiling comes down in front of me.

A spray of embers stings on my face, and I gasp, filling my lungs with burning air and soot. With the ceiling collapsed in front of me, I can't keep moving forward. I have to go back and hope I'll be able to withstand the fire in front of the door. I try to remember if I locked it when Sam and I got here. It might be safer to just jump through the window.

I get back to the stairs at the exact moment the blackened figure steps down onto the bottom step. I recoil from it, but the burning living room stops me from getting more than a few feet away. It turns toward me, and I see Jake's face, blackened skin melting away from the bones of his skull. He takes a step closer, and I lunge out of the way. From this angle, I can see behind him to something stretched out on the stairs. The object that made the thumping sound as he descended. In his hand are thick blond strands matted with blood and ash.

The hair he's using to drag my mother down with him.

Something grabs me from behind, and I scream. But the sound doesn't come out. Instead, my eyes open, and I feel Sam's hand on my shoulder.

"Emma," he says. "Are you alright?"

I look around. Everything is just as it was. My skin feels cool from falling asleep in the air conditioning. I can't smell smoke or hear the angry crackle and hiss of the fire.

My nightmares found me.

"How long have I been asleep?" I ask.

"A little while," Sam tells me. "We were talking, and you just started to fade. You had your head against the side of the couch, so I helped you lie down. It's been about an hour."

"What were we talking about?" I ask.

I pull myself up to sitting and cringe as a sharp pain goes through my head. Pressing the heel of my hand against the pain, I close my eyes.

"The handwriting in the journals and Vincent having this bitter, pushy side no one seems to know. Are you okay? What's wrong?" he asks.

"My head. It really hurts," I tell him.

176

"Do you have any aspirin?"

"There's a bottle on top of the dresser in the bedroom."

"Your old room?" he asks.

"Yes," I say, glad and uncomfortable for the familiarity.

Sam rushes away and a few seconds later comes back with the bottle. He hands it to me so I can shake pills into my palm and gulp down some water.

"What's this?" he asks when I swallow.

I look over, and my heart sinks a little.

"Did you take that out of my room?" I ask.

"It was sitting beside the aspirin, and I was curious about it," he explains.

"It's a thimble," I tell him, trying not to let the defensive anger I feel take over.

I forgot I took it out of the small bag I usually keep it in, so it's sitting on the dresser rather than in my carry on.

"Did you suddenly take up sewing?" he asks.

I give a short laugh and shake my head.

"No. Actually, it's a reminder," I tell him. "When I first went to Feathered Nest and was settling into the cabin, I couldn't open the drawer in the dresser. I found this wedged in the track. Later Jake told me his grandmother collected thimbles. Soon I found out that cabin belonged to his grandmother, so the thimble probably did, too."

Sam looks back at me through darkened eyes.

"It's a reminder of Jake? You keep something with you to remind you of a serial killer who manipulated you and tried to murder you?" he asks, his voice low and gravely.

"No," I tell him. "I need a reminder of what I felt, and the choices I made, so it never happens again."

Sam reaches forward and cups one hand around the side of my face. His thumb brushes over my lips, and I lower my eyes, so I don't see that kiss again. If I don't see it, I won't have to wonder if I want it.

"Sam," I whisper. "I can't." He starts to pull away, and I grab onto his wrist to keep him close. "But will you stay here tonight?"

"Stay here?" he asks.

"I feel safer with you here," I tell him.

He nods. "I'll stay on the couch."

"There's a guest room," I say, but he shakes his head.

"I'd rather be near the door."

He doesn't explain why. He doesn't have to.

CHAPTER THIRTY

S leep eludes me for the rest of the night, so I'm awake when I hear Sam moving around downstairs. A few seconds later, I hear his voice. I can't understand the words he's saying, but he sounds tense and on edge. I slip my feet into a pair of socks to insulate them from the wood steps and make my way down into the living room. He's sitting on the edge of the couch, lacing his boots.

"You need to get in contact with his lawyer and find out what's happening," he says. "This doesn't make any sense at all, and it could be a very serious situation. According to the law, because of the nature of his crime, the jail is under no obligation to inform you of his early release. That's up to him, but the issue is, you are Eva's legal guardians. He can't just reclaim her. Whether he's her father or not, Jimmy is not allowed to just step back in and interfere with the way you're raising Eva. He especially can't just take her away without your permission. I don't know if that's what's happening, but if it is, she's in danger just as she would be with the kidnapper. Maybe not in the same way, but Jimmy isn't prepared or equipped to raise a child. After you've talked to his lawyer, get on the phone with every single friend, associate, contact, and anyone else you can get in touch with, who has

179

had anything to do with Jimmy. We need to find him as quickly as possible. I'll call you later."

He hangs up the call, and I step up closer to him.

"Was that Janet and Paul?" I ask.

"Yes. They needed to know what Pastor Robins said yesterday. Now, he hasn't been in town for as long as most of us, so it's entirely possible he just thought it was Jimmy who showed up at the church looking for Eva. But I find that pretty unlikely."

"Probably just as unlikely as I think it is that Eva isn't one of the kidnapper's victims," I tell him. "Remember the alphabet pattern. She is E and F."

"Gloria should be G and H," he says. "But that didn't stop you from thinking she wasn't kidnapped at all."

"Are you saying you don't suspect Bianca at all now? Her drinking again doesn't make you at all suspicious?"

"I don't know what to think about her. I talked to the hospital, and they confirmed she did work that day, but she left two hours before getting to the community center to pick up Gloria. Not fifteen minutes like she told us. I don't know where she was or what she was doing. But if Gloria fits the alphabet convention and we are still considering the possibility she wasn't kidnapped by the same person, we have to give the same look to all the other children. That means acknowledging the chance Jimmy got out of jail early without telling his parents and came back here to take back his daughter."

He's extremely agitated, his words coming out short and sharp.

"What's going on, Sam? What happened this morning?"

He looks at me for a few seconds, then picks up his phone again and pulls something up on the screen.

"I got an email," he says.

Taking the phone from his hand, I check the sender. It's from Vincent. There's no subject line, but I read the message and feel a shiver move through me.

Out of town with the family, but thought you'd want to see this. If you need to meet, I'll be back Sunday.

I scroll the message down and see he forwarded an email he received early this morning.

There's a picture embedded directly into the body of the email. The image shows a single shoe sitting on a lonely stretch of running track and words written across it in heavy black marker like the one used on the envelopes.

Run, run, as fast as you can.

"He got another clue," I say.

"But this one didn't go to his house. It went to his email, which means whoever's sending these things to him knew he was out of the house and wouldn't find a clue if they just left it sitting there."

"Or that the police are watching the house, and if they got near it again, they'd be seen."

"The handwriting on the picture looks the same as the envelopes and the notes on the papers from the clues leading to Alice Brooks."

I nod. "How about the email address? The one that forwarded this to Vincent?"

"It doesn't have a name attached to it. There aren't any details. The last two times we got clues; they were connected to the children in order of them going missing. First Alice and then Caleb."

"So, the next clue should be for Eva," I say.

"But look at that shoe. That doesn't belong to a ten-year-old girl. It's a guy's shoe. It's hard to tell how big it is because the picture is so close up, but that definitely doesn't belong to her."

"And it being so close up means we can't tell where it is, either," I point out. "Look at the message again. 'Run, run as fast as you can.' Maybe it's still about Caleb? He didn't die. This guy is arrogant. By the time we got to Alice, she had been dead for days. She was already dead by the time he sent the note. So, he decided to up the fun a little for Caleb and make it a race. He didn't think we'd figure it out and find him still alive. Maybe he intends on making sure he doesn't stay that way."

"We need to go talk to Kendra. She's probably at the hospital. She's been staying in the family house next door so she can be as close as possible."

"I'll get dressed."

I hold the phone between my shoulder and ear as I pull on my jeans. It rings three times before the line picks up.

"Hey, Emma. I was wondering why I haven't heard from you. How's Sherwood?" Eric answers.

"I've seen it in better condition. I need you to do something for me. I'm going to forward you an email. It's a forward of another email. Can you find out who sent the original?" I ask.

"Sure."

"Thanks. Is everything okay there?"

"Everything's fine. Your house is still standing and being watched. Creagan is bouncing back and forth between raging against you being insubordinate again to you being the pride of the department depending on who he's talking to."

"Well, that will be fun to deal with when I get back." I pull the phone away from my face long enough to drop a shirt down over my head. "I'll call you soon."

I end the call as I head back into the living room and have Sam forward the email to Eric. I don't hold out a tremendous amount of hope it will be as easy as finding the guy's name attached to the email address, but I have to at least try.

K endra is sitting in the exact same place she was the last time we saw her. The only thing that's changed is her clothing. She's still holding Caleb's hand, and he's still lying still on the bed, looking small and vulnerable. She looks up when we walk in, and her expression is a mix of happiness to see us and the instinctual concern that rises up in a mother when she knows something isn't right.

"What happened?" she asks.

"Kendra, I need you to look at something and tell me if you recognize it," Sam starts.

She nods her agreement, and Sam takes out his phone. He zooms into the image of the shoe and holds it out to Kendra. Stares at it for only a second before shaking her head.

"I don't recognize it. That doesn't belong to Caleb."

"You're sure?" he asks. "Caleb wasn't wearing any shoes when we found him."

"Yes, Sheriff. I know my son's clothes. His shoes might be missing, but that's not one of them. Did this come from the kidnapper?"

"We think so," I say.

"You think he's going to come after my baby again."

"We don't know anything for sure," Sam says. "This just came up, and we're just trying to cover all the bases we can."

"Don't worry," I tell her. "Caleb is safe here. You're here to watch over him, and the staff will take care of him. Let us handle the rest."

We start out of the room, and I look to Sam. "You need to station officers around the hospital. Not just in the parking lot. Inside, preferably on this floor. They need to watch for any visitors who aren't readily recognizable as Caleb's family."

Sam nods, but a desperate scream takes the words he was about to say out of his mouth.

"Help me! Someone, please help me!"

We run toward the sound and see Bianca at the door to the elevator; a little girl draped over her shoulder.

CHAPTER THIRTY-ONE

"Bianca!" Sam shouts and runs toward her.

Her eyes are wild as she looks at him. He gets to her and rests a hand on the girl's back.

"She just showed up at home," Bianca says. "I work a later shift today, and when I was leaving for work, she just stumbled up into the yard and collapsed. Oh, god. What if I had my regular shift? What if I hadn't been there when she got there?"

She turns her sobbing face into Gloria's neck.

"Why didn't you bring her to the emergency room?" Sam asks.

"She's safer in the children's wing. The ER has doors that open right to the outside. What if he comes looking for her?"

It's the type of logic that only makes sense because of the situation, but we aren't going to argue with her. A doctor runs up, and she hands Gloria over to him. The little girl groans, and her eyes flutter open.

"Mama," she says weakly.

"I'm right here, baby. I'm not going anywhere. The doctors are going to take care of you," Bianca whispers through tears.

The doctor and a nurse rush her into a nearby room with Bianca close behind them.

"What do we do now?" I ask.

"We need to talk to her. Until we figure out what this clue is supposed to mean, we don't really have anything to go on. We have to just wait," Sam says.

There's a small waiting room off the side, and he and I go into it. He pulls up the picture of the shoe again and stares at it.

"Click on the image and make it bigger. Maybe there's something in it that we're not noticing," I suggest.

He fills the screen with the image, and we continue to stare at it. I start in one of the top corners of the image and inch my eyes across it, taking in every tiny piece of it individually rather than the entire image. By the time I get to the bottom corner, I haven't found anything new. It's just the shoe with the words written across it.

"It's on a track. Like a running track," Sam says. "But I can't tell where."

"It's outside," I say. "The way the light is hitting it looks like sunlight."

"That means it wasn't taken this morning. It was too cloudy."

"Where are there outdoor running tracks in Sherwood? The middle and high school have them, right?"

"Yes. And the gym. I'll call the station and have people out to those locations to look."

He walks out of the waiting room to make the call, and I stay, sitting in the blue upholstered chair waiting. Waiting for Eric to call and say he found out who the email address is attached to. Waiting for one of the doctors to come in and tell us something. Just waiting.

A few minutes after Sam leaves, Bianca comes into the waiting room. There's a slight awkward tension as she looks at the empty chairs around me.

"Sam had to call up to the station," I tell her. "He should be back any second."

She nods and looks down at her fingers folding and unfolding, twisting her rings in front of her.

"I'm sorry for the way I spoke to you yesterday," she says.

I shake my head and stand up to take a step closer to her. She looks fragile; like any second she might just topple over.

"No," I say. "You don't have to apologize. I..."

"Yes, I do. You're only trying to do your job coming to help us. I shouldn't have reacted like that. I'm still really sensitive talking about my problems. That's something I need to work on. It's just when Sam brought up Holly and her talking about me, it brought up a lot of really bad memories. It frankly scared the hell out of me. I thought back to that day, and I wondered if it was possible that I did go and pick her up somehow and didn't remember. It made me question myself and everything I've been going through to try to be a better person and a better mother. I was so scared that something happened, and I slept or went back to my old habits and somehow that whole section of the day I was blacked out, and I just didn't remember. It was horrible enough to realize my daughter was gone, and I didn't know where she was. But it was even worse to think that maybe somehow, I was the one responsible for it, that I had done something to her or left her somewhere, and whatever she was going through was my fault. I got defensive and angry, and I shouldn't have taken it out on you. I'm sorry."

"Bianca, I have to ask you something," I say gingerly.

This woman is in a delicate situation, and I don't want to make it worse by upsetting her, but I can't just pretend I don't know what Sam told me earlier.

"Alright," she says.

"Sam called the hospital and talked to your supervisor." Her eyes drop to the floor again, and she shifts back and forth on her feet. She knows what I'm about to ask, but she doesn't stop me. "He says she told him you got off two hours before you went to pick up Gloria. You said it was only fifteen minutes. That you just stopped for gas before you went to the community center for her. If that's true, it creates a really big gap. If you did get off when you originally said you did, the sign-out sheet would have Gloria being picked up when you were still at work. But now it has her being picked up while you were off and unaccounted for. Where were you?"

"I didn't do anything to Gloria," she insists. "It scared me, and I started questioning myself, but I didn't do anything to her. I know everything I did that day."

"Then you need to tell us. We need to know the truth."

"Bianca?"

Sam walks into the room behind her, and Bianca turns to look at him.

"She's awake and talking," she tells him. "The doctors have a few exams they want to do, but so far, it seems like she's fine. A few scratches and bruises, but nothing serious."

"I'm so glad to hear that," he tells her.

"Bianca, you need to tell us where you were during those two hours," I say.

She continues to stare at Sam.

"Please," she says, but he shakes his head.

"You do," he tells her. "There's time unaccounted for, and what you were doing during that time could point to who might have had reason to do this."

She lets out a long, defeated breath and sits down heavily in the chair across from me. She pulls her large cross-body bag into her lap and rests her arms on it for a second before digging through it and coming up with a black leather folder.

"I've been struggling with wanting to drink for a couple of months. Things have gotten worse with Gloria's father, and the stress has really been getting to me. I don't ever want to get back to that place again. I don't recognize myself when I'm there. I hate myself. But I know there's always the risk of it happening, and I'm going to have to be the one to stop it. I have to do the work to make sure that I stay in control. So, that's what I've been doing."

My mind goes to the thimble back in its bag, tucked into my carry on.

"What do you mean?" Sam asks.

Bianca unties the leather strips securing the folder closed and pulls out several sheets of thick white cardstock. She holds them out toward us, and I take them.

"What are these?"

"I was at the church fifteen minutes after I left my shift at the hospital. I just wasn't at the community center."

Sam and I look at the papers, and realization settles in.

"You were with the pastor. For counseling."

She nods. "Did you know he's licensed? He says he just does spiritual counseling, but he's just being humble. He became a licensed counselor before he went to seminary. I trust him so much. I've never even considered going to therapy of any kind before, but working with him has really helped. He writes down affirmations for me every time I go in to see him. I bring them around with me everywhere I go, so if I'm starting to feel tempted or overwhelmed, I can look at them, and it makes me feel better. That day I went to my session with him right after I got out of work. He was with someone at the time, an emergency, so I had to wait for a little while before he could see me."

"About how long?" Sam asks.

"Twenty minutes, maybe?"

"Did you see who he was with?"

"Only briefly and not even all of him. I was sitting around the corner waiting, and when I heard Pastor's voice, I went toward the office. The other person was going down the hallway in the other direction, so I only caught part of them going around the corner. It was a man. That's all I know," she says.

"And how long did you meet with Pastor Robins?" I ask.

"Almost an hour."

"So, fifteen minutes after you left work, then another twenty minutes, then another hour. There's still time missing," Sam says.

Bianca nods. "After my session with the pastor, I was still feeling distracted and needed to think through some things. I went into the meditation garden to think about the affirmations he gave me. I do that sometimes."

"These are the affirmations?" I ask.

She nods, and I look down at the papers again. My eyes slide over to Sam, and I find him staring back at me. He sees the same thing. The same heavy, dark ink and blocky letters.

Run, run as fast as you can.

189

CHAPTER THIRTY-TWO

"Baby, Sam's here with his friend Ms. Griffin. They want to talk to you a little bit, okay?" Bianca says, leading us into the room with Gloria.

The little girl is now in a hospital gown covered with a blanket. An IV in her arm pumps fluids just like Caleb, but there doesn't seem to be the same level of desperation. A nurse standing beside the bed is gently cleaning cuts and scrapes along her arm, but Gloria doesn't seem to mind.

"Hi, Gloria," Sam smiles.

Her eyes light up, and she reaches her little hand toward him. He takes it and squeezes as he steps up close enough to run his hand over her thick, dark hair. It's tangled and bits of leaves cling to it, but she looks like she's in fairly good condition.

"Hi, Sam," she says. "Thank you for coming to visit me."

"Of course. I'm here. But I'm not just here to visit you. We need to talk about what happened, okay?"

"Okay," she nods.

There's obvious discomfort and nervousness in her voice, and she glances over at her mother for reassurance.

"You're not in any trouble, sweetheart," Bianca says. "You didn't do anything wrong."

"But I did," Gloria says. "I did do something wrong."

Sam and I look at each other. There are so many questions I want to ask, but I stay back. This little girl is scared and has just gone through something traumatizing. She doesn't know me yet and won't be as willing to open up to me as she will to her mother and a man who she trusts.

"What do you mean? What did you do wrong?" Sam asks.

"I know I'm not supposed to leave the community center without Mama," she says. "I'm supposed to stay inside with everyone else until she comes in, and I walk out with her."

"But that's not what happened," Bianca says.

Gloria shakes her head. "I was excited because I knew she was coming to get me early. I think it was supposed to be a surprise, but Miss Holly let it slip. I was excited to get to spend the day with her. We were going to play, and I was going to ask if we could go have a picnic. I was waiting all morning for her to come. I couldn't even concentrate on my art project. Then it got close to the time when she usually picks me up on her early days, and I started watching the door. I was waiting and waiting and waiting. Then I thought I heard somebody, but I didn't see her. So, when the boys started fighting and Miss Holly was distracted, I went over to the office. We're not supposed to go over there without a grown-up, but I thought maybe Mama was there already, and I just hadn't seen her come in. There wasn't anybody there, but I looked at the sign-out sheet, and she had already signed me out."

"But you didn't see me," Bianca says. "Why would you leave the room without me?"

"Because I saw your name on the sheet. It said you were there and picked me up. I thought maybe somebody had called you, and you went outside to talk. I was going to surprise you by coming out to you because you always come in for me. So, I got all my stuff and left. I didn't say anything to Miss Holly because I knew she would stop me if she didn't see you. I didn't want her with me when I came outside. I know the two of you don't like each other very much, and I just wanted it to be us. I'm sorry, Mama."

She hangs her head, and Bianca steps past Sam to wrap her hands around her little daughter's face and kiss her over and over on her forehead and cheeks.

"Don't cry, baby. Don't cry. I'm not upset with you. Miss Holly and I like each other just fine. I'm sorry you felt that way."

"I just wanted to surprise you."

Bianca tilts Gloria's face up so she can look into her huge, dark eyes. "And I love that."

"Who was outside when you got out there?" Sam asks.

"I don't know," Gloria says.

"What do you mean?" Bianca asks. "You got in the car with a stranger?"

"I didn't mean to. I went outside to look for you and didn't see you. There wasn't anyone at the desk, so I couldn't ask where you were. I walked a little bit down the sidewalk, and then I thought maybe something bad happened, and you had to go back to the hospital. I was going to go back inside, but then someone grabbed me. I couldn't see anything, and I tried to scream, but they shoved something in my mouth."

Bianca's face falls. "I heard her. Oh, god. I heard her. I was sitting in the meditation garden, and I heard a sound. It was like a scream, but it was so short, and I didn't hear anything after it. I thought maybe it was a bird or an animal. I heard her, and I didn't know. I'm so sorry."

"It's not your fault," Gloria says, taking her turn to comfort her crying mother.

"The person who grabbed you, were they tall? Short? Heavy? Could you tell anything about them?"

"Not really," Gloria says. "I was so scared I couldn't really pay attention. They were strong enough to pick me up and put me in the back of a car."

"Okay. Then what happened? How long were you in the car?"

"A long time. But it felt like we were going around in circles. Like we weren't really going anywhere. Then it got really bumpy for a while, and we stopped. The person got me out of the car and made me climb up a ladder."

"A ladder?" Sam asks.

"Yeah. But not a real one. Just little pieces of wood nailed into the side of a tree. They put me in a treehouse at the top and told me when I heard the car leave; I could take the blindfold off."

"What did their voice sound like?" Bianca asks.

"Like they were talking through a tunnel," Gloria says.

"They were using a voice modifier," Sam says. "What was in the treehouse?"

"A chalkboard. Pens and paper. Some books. A few bottles of water and some crackers and stuff."

"Did the person come back?"

"No. I was there all by myself, and I was really scared. It wasn't like a normal treehouse. There was a big door, and it was locked. But I wanted to get out. I wanted to come home. I broke the wood over the window and crawled out."

"You escaped," Bianca says.

Gloria nods. "I ran and tried to remember how to get back. It took all night, but I got home."

"Yes, you did," Bianca whispers, kissing her again. "You're such a brave girl."

"You did an amazing job," Sam tells her. "I know it was dark, and you were really scared, but do you think you could get us back to the treehouse?"

Gloria nods.

"Does she really have to?" Bianca asks. "It was so horrible for her. Does she really have to go back there?"

"We need to see it. It's possible this guy put the other children there, too, before… We just need to see it and search the area. Eva is still missing, and she's next in line."

"I can do it," Gloria says.

"Good girl," he says, then looks at Bianca. "The doctors will probably want to keep her for a little longer just to make sure she's alright.

Emma and I will go get all the supplies we need; then we'll be back here. Stay strong. Your baby is here. She's doing just fine. Now we have one more to go."

Bianca nods. We walk out of the room and cross the wing to Caleb's room again.

"Is everything alright?" Kendra asks. "What's happening?"

"Gloria Hernandez is here. She's alive."

"Oh, thank God," Kendra gasps, pressing her hand to her heart. "Where was she? Where'd they find her?"

"We didn't find her. She escaped. Kendra, I need you to think about what the doctors have told you about Caleb's condition. Did they mention any injuries like cuts or scrapes?"

"He had a few on his arms and legs. But his hands." She turns one of his hands over in her palm and strokes it with her fingertips. "They were full of splinters."

"He was kept there, too," I say.

"Kept where?" Kendra asks.

"Gloria was able to give us some information about where the kidnapper brought her. It seems they were kept in a treehouse. Does that sound familiar?"

She shakes her head. "I don't know of any treehouse that's not in somebody's backyard."

"Okay. If you can think of anything else, call me," Sam says.

We head out of the room, and my phone rings as we ride the elevator down.

"Eric?" I answer. "Did you find out who that email belongs to?"

"Yes. In a way," he says.

"What does that mean?"

We hurry across the parking lot and get into Sam's car.

"It seems to be a burner email. It was only registered a few days ago, and the only activity has been that one email."

"What's the name that registered it?" I ask.

"Samuel Johnson."

CHAPTER THIRTY-THREE

My head swims, and I can hear blood rushing in my ears. I squeeze my eyes closed and try to take deep breaths to keep my stomach settled.

"Emma? Emma, it's not him. You know it's not him," Eric says.

"I know," I manage to get out. "It's just bad memories."

"Is there anything else I can do?" he asks.

"No. Thank you."

I hang up and look over at Sam.

"What's wrong?" he asks.

"The email address that sent that clue to Vincent this morning is registered to you," I tell him.

His eyes widened, and his face goes dark.

"Emma, you know…"

"I know it wasn't you," I tell him. "You were with me when a lot of this was happening. This person is taunting you. They're calling you out. Something else is going to happen, and we need to figure it out before it does."

"As soon as the doctors will let her, we will take Gloria out and have her show us to this treehouse." He hesitates for a second. "The handwriting on those affirmations Bianca showed us. You saw it, too."

"It's the same as the clues," I confirm.

"But the pastor was with Bianca when Gloria was taken from the community center," he points out.

"No. Bianca was in the meditation garden. We don't know where Pastor Robins was."

Sam looks at me with eyes that hope I have more to say, but I don't.

We have to wait two more hours before the doctor clears Gloria to come with us. I'm nervous as we get into the car with her. She's still very young, and children, especially children who went through an emotional and physical trauma like being kidnapped and held for two days, aren't known for being especially reliable.

Sometimes they are able to do incredible things and remember every single detail about what happened. But sometimes they get fundamental things wrong. Mary Katherine Smart watched her sister Elizabeth be abducted, but later described the man to the police with completely incorrect details, from the color he was wearing to saying he had on a golf hat. But in the end, they found Elizabeth, so I have to have as much faith in Gloria as I can.

The path she takes us on is long and winding, starting at her house and leading us backwards along the way she came. It takes us deep into the woods more than half a mile from her neighborhood and then through the trees, thorns, and thick brush. There are many times when she stops and looks around like she's not sure where she is or what she's supposed to do next. I can't push her. Sam is there beside her, and she's trusting him, one hand tucked inside his as we walk.

Bianca agreed to stay with one of the cars securing the entrance to the woods and wait for us. Sam didn't want too many people muddying the waters of Gloria's thoughts or making her nervous. As vital as it is for children to be protected and advocated for in difficult situations, it's also a reality that most respond better and are more willing to open up when they don't have the pressure of a parent right there.

Finally, she stops. Her empty hand lifts, trembling as she points ahead of us.

"There," she says.

I follow her finger and see the dark form of an old treehouse built into the frame of several thick oak branches several yards away. Sam reaches for his gun and hands Gloria behind him to me.

"Stay with Emma, okay? If she tells you to run, you need to do what she says."

Gloria nods and backs up to me. I wrap my arms around her shoulders, so she feels surrounded by me. Holding his weapon ready in front of him, Sam approaches the treehouse. He demands anyone inside to announce themselves. There's only silence.

He shouts again. When there's no movement or response, he puts his gun away and climbs up the pieces of wood nailed into the side of the tree, just like Gloria described. Pulling himself up onto the small platform in front of the door, Sam puts one hand on his gun again and uses the other to turn the knob. My arms tighten around Gloria as he throws open the door and draws his gun in the same movement. He pauses, then steps inside. An instant later, he emerges again.

"It's empty," he calls down.

He takes out his radio and calls for some of the officers at the edge of the woods to come in. They will take Gloria to Bianca, then bring both of them back to the station for some more questions while we examine the treehouse and the surrounding area.

When Gloria is safely gone, I climb up into the treehouse. The wood of the steps presses into my hands, and when I grab for the edge of the platform, I feel the slice of a splinter sliding into my skin. It makes me think of the children and what they went through right here. A treehouse is supposed to be fun, an escape into their own world where they can play and think, imagine, and relax. It's not supposed to be a place of terror and isolation.

I get inside the treehouse and look around. The floor of one corner is scattered with papers, pens, and crayons. Without touching any of them, I look down at the papers and see what the children drew and wrote.

Help me.

Dear Mama.

Caleb was here.

Sam points out empty water bottles and bags of snacks in another corner.

"There isn't enough here for it to be from all the children," he notes. "The kidnapper must have cleaned up after each child and prepared for the next one."

"Why? What would be the point of that? If they're going to hold these children captive and eventually kill them, why try to make them comfortable?" I ask.

"So, they will last longer?"

Hanging on one wall, I see the chalkboard Gloria described. On the car ride over, she told us it was like one a friend of hers had in her treehouse. They used it to play school. The thought runs through my mind that this one looks like it was once used for the same purpose. Then I realize what I'm looking at, and my heart drops.

"Sam," I say, pointing to the chalkboard.

"It's the alphabet," he says.

"Right. Do the letters look familiar to you?"

He pulls out his phone and compares images of the clues to the letters written across the board in white chalk.

"They look alike," he says.

My heart drums in my chest so hard I can hear it.

"Sam, look at the letters." Some of the letters are crossed out the way a teacher does while teaching small children to write letter by letter. But these aren't random. I move my finger along the board, pointing to the crossed-out letters. "A, B. Alice Brooks. C, D. Caleb Donahue. E,F. Eva Francis. G,H. Gloria Hernandez. I, J."

Our eyes meet.

"There's another one," he says. "Another child is missing."

"Run, run, as fast as you can," I murmur.

The next several hours are a flurry of names, school records, and phone calls. Every available officer scours pages and makes phone calls, checking on the children who match the right age range and have names that fit the alphabet order. Any child between the ages of ten and eleven with first and last names that start with I and J are on our list. Every call gets shorter, every check-in with a parent, babysitter, grandparent, or summer-school teacher more desperate. Finally, Sam bursts into the room where I'm hunched over a table looking at the journals, papers, and clues again.

"We got the name," he says. "Isaac Jacobs. Ten years old. He was last seen this morning when his parents left for work, leaving him at home with his older sister. She went out with her boyfriend even though she wasn't supposed to. Says she left around ten. His parents called to check on him at eleven but didn't ask to talk to the sister. When they got our call, they called their daughter, and she went home to find him missing."

"And..." I lead.

"He plays for the youth soccer team at the church," he says.

"Shit," I say in a gust of breath.

"We need to reach out to the parents of any child in that age range and make sure they keep them close. He's moving faster now, and the next child could get taken at any time."

"You're right," I say. "Start with K, L. They're next in line. Any child between ten and eleven with those initials need to be kept at home with constant adult supervision until this is over."

Sam starts to walk out of the room, but stops, his head lifting, and then frantic eyes turning to me.

"Vincent," he says.

"What about Vincent?"

"Vincent Lam. His son."

"Singer?" I ask.

"That's just what they call him. His name is Kessinger."

CHAPTER THIRTY-FOUR

"Answer your fucking phone!" Sam shouts, hitting the button to end his fifth call to Vincent.

My phone rings in my ear. My third call to Valerie. Suddenly, it picks up.

"Hello?" she says.

"Valerie, it's Emma Griffin."

"What do you want?" she asks, the breeziness of her answer gone from her voice as soon as she hears my name.

"When are you coming home from your trip?" I ask.

"Tomorrow. Why? Do you need me there to dig through my house and humiliate my family more?" she snaps.

"No. I need you and Vincent to keep Singer away for as long as you can," I tell her.

"Vincent? What do you mean?"

"We have reason to believe it's not safe for your son to be in Sherwood right now. You and Vincent need to keep him away until you hear from us again," I explain.

"Singer is in Sherwood," she says.

"What?"

"He's at home. He and Vincent didn't come with me on this trip. I'm visiting my sister like I do every summer. What's going on?"

"You need to get home as soon as you can," I say and end the call before she can respond.

"What's wrong?" Sam asks.

"We need to go. Right now."

We run out to the car, and I snatch the keys from him so I can drive. I can't sit and do nothing right now, even for the few minutes it will take to get to the Lam house.

"Vincent and Singer never left Sherwood. They didn't go with Valerie. They've been here the whole time."

"Oh, no."

The door to the car doesn't close behind me when I jump out, but I don't bother to go back and close it. I run up the sidewalk as fast as I can and yank at the door. It's locked, but not secure enough to withstand Sam's boot slamming into the lock and his shoulder splintering the center. We run inside, screaming for Vincent and Singer. The silence that echoes back at us sends cold sweat down the back of my neck.

"Let's go upstairs," I say.

"Shit," Sam mutters as we run toward the upstairs hallway, where I assume the family bedrooms are. "Why didn't I think about Singer? Why didn't it ever occur to me?"

One by one, we check every inch of the rooms upstairs but find no sign of Vincent or Singer. I open the last door, and a burst of white-hot memory sears across the back of my eyes. I squeeze my eyes closed, ridding my thoughts of the images from Jake's basement, and open them again to see the fresh blood. It soaks into the pale rug positioned under the bed and stains the white comforter beneath Vincent's body. His phone sits beside him, and a knife is on the floor directly beneath the hand hanging over the edge of the bed.

Sam runs up to the bed and presses his fingers to the side of Vincent's neck.

"He's alive," he says. "His pulse is weak, but he's alive. Call an ambulance."

I run back out of the room as I call for the EMS. As I'm talking to them, I search every other room, closet, and corner of the house. The basement door mocks me. It dares me to open it. I call its bluff and take the narrow wooden stairs three at a time to get to the cement floor below faster.

It's chilly down here, even with the summer heat outside. Boxes and plastic totes piled along the walls are carefully arranged by season or holiday. Everything is perfectly labeled, organized to exacting precision. The labels tell the story of which member of the family packed which, though I have no doubt the positioning of the boxes was already thoroughly planned before a single item went inside.

Vincent labeled the boxes for Easter and Halloween.

A messy, childlike hand-marked boxes of sports equipment and winter clothing.

Valerie's smooth script is idyllic Christmas movie perfection on boxes of ornaments and lawn decorations.

I stop in the middle of the floor, staring at the stack in front of me. I reach out to touch the label before I think about the possibility of fingerprints.

Valentine's Day.

The sound of sirens overhead draws me back up the stairs and to the front door. I direct the team of emergency responders up the stairs and stumble outside. A car skids to a stop across the street, and Jennings hops out. I stalk up to him to stop him from running into the house.

"Where is she?" he demands. I notice he doesn't have his camera in his hands. "Where's Valerie?"

"Back up, Jennings. You can't go in there," I say.

"Where is Valerie?" he asks again. "Why is there an ambulance here? Is she alright?"

"What are you doing here? How would you know something was going on?"

"I have a police scanner in my car. I heard the address."

I've heard that excuse before, and hearing it again makes a metallic taste rise up the back of my throat.

"You need to leave. Your little game is over," I tell him.

"What game?" he asks.

The rattle of the stretcher behind me makes me move out of the way, and I look to the side to see Vincent's bloodied body strapped down, and a responder frantically pumping an oxygen bulb over his face to keep him alive.

"You can't honestly think I would have anything to do with this," he says. "I might have come up with a million different ways to get Vincent Lam out of my life, but I'd never do something like this."

"Not even to impress Valerie?"

He didn't hurt the children. I know he didn't. But there's something I need to hear from him.

"I would do anything for her. I love Valerie. I have for years. There was a time when I really thought we would be together, but she wouldn't leave Vincent. She said it would look too bad. She couldn't stand going through a divorce. Having that label. But I couldn't just have an affair with her that would last into perpetuity without any thought that maybe someday we'd actually be together. I hated sneaking back and forth to Sherwood and only getting bits and pieces of her. I want her to myself. That's the reason I was so excited about this story. If I could impress her with the fame and success an exclusive on a story like this would bring, she would finally know I'm the one she's supposed to be with."

"Then you found out about the clues being sent to Vincent," I say.

He holds up his hands innocently. "I had nothing to do with that. It sickened me to think about Vincent being the one to hurt those kids, but..."

"It also meant he would be gone soon, and you could stake your claim on Valerie again."

"Yes," he says aggressively. "Is that what you wanted to hear? If he had finally cracked and was making all this shit up so he could finally get the push he wanted into being a big name, she wouldn't have any reason to stay with him. But I didn't do this. I talked to her yesterday, and she said she wasn't going to divorce him. Even with all this, she wasn't going to."

Sam comes out of the house behind me and immediately descends on Jennings, but I push him back with a glare.

"We need to go to the station," I tell him. "I need to look at the evidence we took from here again."

A squad car pulls up to the front of the house, and officers emerge to start processing the scene. I push Sam away from Jennings, but he resists long enough to stick a finger in the man's face.

"Get away from here. I don't want to see a single word of any of this printed. You already fucked up bad, and I'm just looking for any excuse to wipe the floor with you," he growls.

Sam's shaking as we drive to the station, pedal to the floor and blowing through stoplights with a siren on.

"He knew we were getting close. We were right all along and were going to figure out that he did all this. His son was the tipping point, and he tried to kill himself to cover it up."

"He's alive, Sam. And he's going to talk," I say.

We get back to the station, and I go directly to the room I have spread with all the papers, notebooks, clues, and books. I look at each one of them, noting the time they were written and what was happening in the ones I could identify. Sam has to meet with the rest of the task force to check on their progress with the children still missing and how he is going to move the investigation forward. I stay in the room, walking around the table, my mind going a hundred different directions, and yet always coming back to the same thing.

I take out my phone and send Sam a text.

We were wrong.

Making sure the GPS is activated on my phone, I take a picture of the map of Sherwood with notations of where the children went missing and where they were found and run out of the station.

CHAPTER THIRTY-FIVE

Fear threatens to keep me away. It drags me, pulling me backwards as I try to make my way through the woods. I parked as close as I could, but the old access road is closed, forcing me to walk the rest of the way. Every step gets harder as panic builds in my stomach and crawls up my throat. It blurs my eyes and burns at the tips of my ears. My hands tingle, and my legs sting. My body is doing everything it can to keep me in place, to stop me from going any further.

But it's not fear of what is ahead of me. It's fear of what's behind me. I remember each step through the woods behind the cabin. I remember the crunch of the leaves and hearing steps coming toward me through darkness I couldn't penetrate. I dove into the danger, into the unknown, and I'm going to do it again. This time there's more at stake. Three children are still missing. One is dead, another still barely clinging to life, another with damage she will carry with her every day. I carry my own damage in my heart, in the back of my mind, and on my hand. I can't take their burden from them, but I can stop it from getting worse.

Twilight fills the spaces between the trees as I make my way through them. Thank god for long summer evenings and the pureness of moonlight. I don't want to think of any of those children passing a night in the darkness.

The walk isn't as long as it feels, and my feet finally follow the end of the access road to what used to be a parking lot. It's broken and overgrown now, only small bits of the blacktop visible through the tall grass and small trees that have overtaken it. I cross over it toward the hulking building. It looks more frightening in the half-light, but seeing it makes hope rise in my chest. I didn't know for sure it would still be here, that it was still standing. I've only seen it once, many years ago, when it wasn't in as bad of condition as it is now, and there were more people around me to take away the edge of foreboding.

The old school hasn't been open in decades. Its square brick structure and large steps leading up to the front door hearken to another time when children flocked in their nicest clothing and the pursuit of good grades was paramount. Not like it is now. The hallways of schools have changed. The people who come out of them changed for it.

I walk past the dirty white stone steps and the boarded-up front door to the crumbled sidewalk leading around to the back of the school. Down the slight slope at the back is one of the modern additions added to the grounds during the last-gasp years of the school. A playground has been broken down to its skeleton, swings gone, jungle gym dismantled, only metal frames and a slide visible against the horizon. The only time I came here, that playground rang with the sound of preteen laughter.

We shouldn't have been here. I was barely old enough to be out of the house by myself and should have been afraid the moment the older kids led us into the woods and brought us here. But Sam was there. Older and more confident, a leader even when he didn't realize it. He ushered me here, and we ran around the ruins of the school grounds, laughing for no reason, relishing the freedom, wanting it to never end.

Beyond the playground, a running track added for the short time this school was converted into a private high school winds in a circle against the grass. I can't see it, but I can make a guess if I go down there, I'll find a shoe sitting on it.

I turn back around and head for the rear of the school. The doors are boarded up, but there's a broken window. Several of the panes have been removed, and the glass smoothed to create an easy entrance for anyone willing to make the climb. I do and drop down onto the dusty floor of the school's gym. Footprints mar the thick dirt coating the once-polished floor, and I follow them, letting them bring me to the doors at the end that open out into the hallway. The rusted hinges of the door scream loudly as I push the door open, but I don't care. Let them hear me. Let them come.

I've only taken a few steps through the shadowy space illuminated only by the evening light filtering in when I see movement ahead of me. A figure steps into view. The black silhouette makes my palms sweat as my nightmare replays in my mind. But it isn't the grotesque burned image of Jake coming toward me. I hold my ground, steadying my stance.

"How's your sister?" I call into the darkness. "You certainly got back into town fast."

"You shouldn't have come here," Valerie says, stepping into the light of the window several feet behind me.

"No, Valerie, you shouldn't have come here. Do you know how close we came to arresting Pastor Robins? Not something I'd think you would want for someone you love."

Her face falls. "Patrick? Is he alright?"

"He's fine. I can't say the same for after we tell him about all this. And your husband is alive, by the way. You didn't do very well staging his suicide. Never slice across the wrist. Always down it. You've read far too many books. Speaking of which, did you get the idea from the book, or did the book speak to you because it was your life? That one with the inscription I found in your bedroom? You picked it off the shelf the day we were there to talk to Vincent about the clues. The one leading to the second child you tried to kill."

She stiffens. "I don't know what you're talking about."

"Of course you do. *Fracture*. That's a tough one. I've read it. Can't say I got quite the same thing out of it that you did. The woman who thought she was living her perfect life until she fell in love with someone else and lived out her life with both; her daily life devoted to her husband and her longing passion for her lover keeping her life interesting. A bit of a cliché, but with a bit of a twist, I guess. That's why you could never divorce Vincent for William Jennings. You felt like you needed to have both in order to fulfill you. But here's the thing. You don't care about Jennings anymore. He's behind you because you found someone else who is even more desirable and even more blissfully unattainable. Here's my question... do you always realize when you're writing in someone else's handwriting?"

Valerie's eyes narrow. "Bianca's was easy. It looks like a preteen girl's. And even if I got it slightly wrong, everyone would just think she was drunk."

"I'm not talking about Bianca." The smug look falls from her face. "Those notebooks we took from your house. I thought they were all written by Vincent. It looked like he was losing touch with reality. Just scribbling down whatever came to mind. But that's not what they were. They weren't a journal or a novel. They were from your couples' therapy with Pastor Robins. He wanted the two of you to learn to communicate better with each other by writing to each other. But by that point, Vincent wasn't even a person to you anymore. He was an idea. The husband who lived day to day life with you, but could never give you the true, passionate love you believe can only be attained when you can't be with someone every day. In your mind, you embodied Vincent, you created a narrative, and it played out when you wrote back to him in those books. Your handwriting became like his. Just like your handwriting became like the pastor's when you were thinking of him. You became so enmeshed with this idea of your forbidden love that if you let yourself think about him, you started to write in his handwriting."

"How would I know his handwriting that well?" she spits.

"The affirmations he writes down for you during your private sessions. He does the same for Bianca Hernandez. But I'm sure you know that. Every child you chose had a connection to the pastor. Was that part of your plan? You were going to keep kidnapping and killing them until we finally arrested Vincent, then you were going to fall into the arms of Pastor Robins? You would comfort each other, and then you'd finally have the passion you've been aching for? But you could never have him as your husband. He already has a wife and a child. He would be your secret, and you his. It's unfortunate you couldn't stop thinking about him enough to not write in his hand-writing when you wrote the clues. He almost went down for the crimes you committed."

Valerie lunges at me, and I latch onto her in midair. She punches me, and I knee her in the stomach, disabling her long enough to get to my feet. She clamps onto me again, and I knock her to the ground, landing on her with my knee in her chest. She tries to buck me off, but I grab onto the front of her shirt to stop her. One final flail of her body slams her head onto the ground, and her eyes flutter closed.

I can already hear the sirens outside. Sam's here.

It's over.

EPILOGUE

"How could you possibly have figured that out?" Vincent asks.

It's been two days since Sam pulled me off Valerie on the floor of the old school, and I'm at the hospital doing my rounds to check on everyone. Vincent is sitting up in his bed, much of the color back in his face. Both arms are tightly wrapped in gauze, and a bandage stretches across his neck and chest.

"Her obsession with books and words," I tell him. "She wasn't living in reality. Everything was crafted like she was living a book in her own head. The names being in the order of the alphabet was a nod to Agatha Christie. The way she worded things in your notebooks was straight out of books and plays. She'd slipped out of real-life and into something she made for herself. Her handwriting changed depending on who she was creating at that moment. She was obsessed with Pastor Robins, believing he was her answer to love and devotion, made passionate and enticing because it was completely forbidden and impossible. When she was thinking about him and the love affair she was designing in her head, her handwriting slipped into his. She stared at those affirmations so many times; it was as much a part of

215

her as her own. It really hit me when I went into the basement at your house and saw the labels on the different boxes. Valerie organized and controlled everything. It all had to be exactly perfect, which is why everything is stacked how she wants it. But you each labeled things, right?"

"Yes. That happened after our basement flooded about a year ago. We had to clean it out completely, reseal it, then organize it again. She divided up the tasks, and we all labeled what we packed."

"And she was responsible for Christmas and Valentine's Day," I say. "Right."

"Valentine's Day was written in Pastor Robin's handwriting," I tell him.

He nods painfully. "I went to see him. I found the affirmations and recognized the handwriting. I didn't even know she was doing private sessions with him. So, I went to confront him."

"And he told you he didn't have anything to do with the children or with your wife."

"Yes. I didn't know what it meant, but I talked to Valerie about it," he says.

"And that's when she realized she was going to have to speed things along and have you kill yourself out of the tremendous guilt of the horrible things you did," I continue. "Bianca saw you leaving the office. She didn't know it was you, but it gave me a clue."

"Emma."

I turn to the door and see Sam standing there. I smile at Vincent and walk out into the hallway.

"He's awake," Sam says.

I hurry behind him to the elevator and ride it up to the children's wing. We rush into the room and see Caleb reclined in his bed, eating a container of blue Jell-O. Kendra sits at the side of the bed, still gripping his hand, tears sliding down her cheeks.

"Look at you," Sam smile.

"Caleb, this is Emma," Kendra says, pointing at me. "She's the lady who saved you."

"Thank you," he says around a mouthful of blue.

I choke back unexpected tears.

"Thank you for being so strong."

After a few minutes of visiting with Caleb, we go down the hall to Eva, who's sitting up in bed with her grandparents on either side and her father stretched out beside her. Jimmy was the surprise at the school. I was expecting to find the missing children in one of the classrooms, but I didn't think I'd also find him, handcuffed to a radiator, wearing only one shoe.

Valerie took him when she showed up to the house to get Eva and found Jimmy there with her. He fought to protect his daughter. Valerie was just faster. She knocked him off the porch and grabbed Eva. He followed them all the way to the school, still locked in his distrust of the police that would hopefully fade with time out in the world. That's where Valerie got the jump on him. She was just strong enough to drag him into the classroom.

Isaac and Singer were both released from the hospital yesterday. Neither were seriously injured and hadn't been with Valerie long enough to get as dehydrated and hungry as the others. The cleaned-up water bottles and snacks make sense. A mother wouldn't want children to suffer. Even children she planned to kill. Especially her own child.

We walk out of the hospital, and Sam suddenly stops me, taking both of my hands in his.

"What now?" he asks.

I let out a sigh.

"Now I do a lot of paperwork, which is seriously the last thing I ever want to do."

"I mean, after the case is over. Do you have to go back now?"

"Actually, I've been thinking about taking a leave of absence. I think I need some time away from the office."

And the tension still surrounding my house, but I don't mention that.

"Where will you go?"

"I know this place. It's really sweet and has a house with pink azaleas in the yard. It's also close enough for me to get back to the office if I really need to. I might hang out there for a while. If that's okay with the sheriff in town."

He smiles at me.

"That's more than okay."

I see that kiss again, and as I tilt my mouth up to take it, my phone rings. He cringes, and I laugh.

"The real world calls." I click the button to answer. "Hey, Bells."

"I am supposed to be bringing your mail in this time, right?" she asks.

"Yes. And I might actually be asking you to bring it in for a while longer."

"That's fine. I just wanted you to know you got a package today," she says.

"Oh, that must be what Clancy found. What's in it?"

Sam reaches out to put his hand on my hip, and I relax into the touch as I listen to the sound of Bellamy tearing into something.

"Oh, it's pretty. But I don't really recognize it. Let me send you a picture."

My phone beeps to announce the arrival of the picture, and I pull it away from my ear to see the image. My mouth goes dry, and my hand clamps down on Sam's shirt.

It's a necklace. Exactly like the one in the box with the birthday note.

THE END

Dear Reader,

Thank you for your continued support. I really appreciate that you read the second book in my series!

I hope you liked this book just as much as *The Girl in Cabin 13*.
If you can please leave me a review for this book as well, I would
appreciate that enormously.
Your reviews allow me to get the validation I need to keep going as an
indie author.
Just a moment of your time is all that is needed.

Again, thank you for reading *The Girl That Vanished*.
I promise to always do my best to bring you thrilling adventures.

Yours,
A.J. Rivers

P.S. Checkout Book 3 - The Girl in the Manor on the next page!

P.S.S. If for some reason you didn't like this book or found typos or
other errors, please let me know personally. I do my best to read and
respond to every email at aj@riversthrillers.com

The Girl in the Manor is the thrilling and addictive third novel in A.J.
Rivers' Emma Griffin FBI Series.

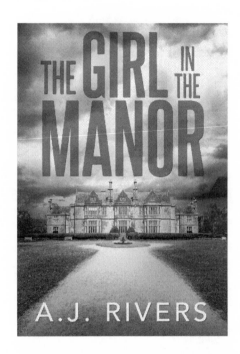

What mysteries lie behind the disturbing death of the girl in the manor?

Order you copy now from your to find out.

STAYING IN TOUCH WITH A.J.

Type the link below in your internet browser now to join my mailing list and get your free copy of Edge Of The Woods.

https://dl.bookfunnel.com/ze03jzd3e4

MORE EMMA GRIFFIN FBI MYSTERIES

Emma Griffin's FBI Mysteries is the new addictive best-selling series by A.J. Rivers. Make sure to get them all below!

Visit my author page on Amazon to order your missing copies now! Now available in paperback!

ALSO BY A.J. RIVERS

The Girl and the Deadly End
The Girl and the Hunt
The Girl and the Deadly Express
The Girl Next Door
The Girl in the Manor
The Girl That Vanished
The Girl in Cabin 13
Gone Woman

Made in the USA
Middletown, DE
27 April 2024

53562054R00137